The Intersection of Daydream and Driving Slow

Also by Penny Sidoli
_____

The Last Bear in Santa Barbara

The Intersection of Daydream and Driving Slow

Short Stories

Penny Sidoli

Copyright ©2014 by Penny Sidoli

All names, characters, places and incidents are the product of the author's imagination or are used fictitiously. Any resemblance to current events, locales or incidents is entirely coincidental.
All rights reserved.

Cover Photo and interior photos
by Penny Sidoli

Book typeface Plantagenet Cherokee

Printed in the United States of America
by CreateSpace

ISBN 13: 978-1502433442
ISBN 10: 1502433443

www.pennysidoli.com

CONTENTS

THE SOUTHWEST

Extraordinary (Rock) 1

A Brand New Cadillac 14

Josie Goes West 19

Reno Silver 22

Sheila's Only The Lonely Butte 42

Wild Release 51

This Is A Remember When Story 77

THE NORTHWEST

A Bird 90

Comet 94

White Skiff 108

Spirit Chief 122

THE SOUTHWEST

EXTRAORDINARY (ROCK)

    Carola pushed the forms away, her concentration shattered by the noise of brakes squealing and gears grinding as the afternoon school bus stopped at the row of mailboxes to discharge its group of fluttering birds, the children. After the yellow beast roared away, the dust settled and the children's yelling voices faded into the distance, she remained irritated. She gave up trying to find her train of thought, gave up on a pen that had run out of ink, left her shady patio and walked out to the gate. Blue went with her, and she grew calmer as she petted him and scratched his white muzzle. Side by side at the gate they studied their landscape as the desert released its secrets one quiet movement at a time, a tortoise emerging beneath brush, prairie dogs popping their heads out of a fresh hole, soaring turkey vultures, endless secret territories.
    Carola's gaze took in a whole mountain in the distance, her special mountain, dark grey, volcanic and immense, wonderful. Her focus drifted along its sky-edged rimline down to the faint scratch of a distant road that she knew well. The road led over the mountain's backside to their mine. Her gaze slipped back to her own ten acres. The sacahuistas were blooming. She had modeled those tiny pale bud clusters

many times in her silverwork jewelry, sculpted and adorned with white opal, garnet and blue opal gemstones. Her other favorites were the sage, ocotillo, and saguaro cactus. She had absorbed all their qualities, found them all handily from the top of the mountain all the way down to their ten acres that now as Mark's widow were her ten acres. For many years she drew the shapes, inhaled their scents, studied and stylized them into jewelry that sold well and gave them income enough to call their ten acres a home.

She was left now to handle everything alone, chores, upkeep, forms. She had to push through torpor to shift her attitude into affirmation. They gave her a house and loving kindness for a large part of her life and a short section of theirs. The mental shift came as stubborn as the gears of the school bus. Something today not just the school bus had twisted her peace, wrenched her out of calm into a struggle against bitterness.

Their prospecting permit renewal had arrived yesterday in its official envelope. As she stood at the gate, inert, staring at the lumps and bumps of her memories on a mountain, half the form remained blank. Sometimes she felt him nearby; not now, and yet she yearned. Was it whimsy or mystery? Mark would have filled out that form in a few minutes and gone down to the mailbox, flipped up the red metal arm, snapped the lid closed, and whistled his way home, making footprints on the dusty road.

She could not finish that form; she could not fill in all the blanks. Or maybe she just plain didn't like the decision she was coming to. Looking again for the faint road to the mine, she loathed that others might figure out what they did and go look for an exposed basalt dike rich with opal as blue as fallen pieces of sky. Once she let go, the mine would be gone forever, never getting it back.

Officially it was a bunch of prospect holes on the side of a certain little steep hill, far back in the wilderness of a dry range. They had to restore those exploratory digs by terms of the prospecting permit, filling in the holes after hammering, chipping, and hauling out the best ore. That's the work they'd done for years together, plus the three years she tried her best at it, just Carola and Chips, and maybe not even three counting the time out for Chips to build the house, maybe a couple trips before Chips gave out and she gave up. He didn't have Mark's gusto. He had been Mark's best friend and may have taken it on with her as a way to tag along. The last trip was pretty bleak in takings. Chips had no focus. He would have been content to wander the hills until he got hungry for a meal, goofy and aimless. For her, the fact to face was that mining as an endeavor was finished and done. Those permit renewal papers waited behind her on the patio table, a hunk of opal ore holding them down. She hadn't sold a single piece of jewelry for a year, the year since Chips killed himself. He had been tremendous after Mark's sudden death. The second time losing a partner felt like being hit by a rock avalanche.

She had bought gemstones from prospectors before marrying Mark and she could do it again after Chip's death. She had to admit that she didn't care about the mine. That was the decision, to let go of the prospecting permit, but not the root of what bothered her. She had to dig deep inside herself to pull that up.

The opal oozed up as a hot liquid along a vertical crack that brought the lava close to the surface and spilled it out into the air like a long tongue, otherwise she and Mark would have been digging hundreds of feet straight down to get the good stuff. The particular rock they wanted, blue opal, was in gorgeous layers, fused together while liquid, like batter in a marble cake.

To get the ore required back-breaking rock smashing. She and Mark had done that, and it killed him. Day after day spent digging and drilling holes, hitting the rock with heavy iron wedges and a huge maul hammer called 'the stupid stick'; and picking up the broken pieces of rock, putting them into backpacks, fifty, sixty pounds of rock each, carrying them three miles to the truck. Once they took double loads each on three trips and afterward she and Mark stayed in bed for more than a week recuperating. They weren't as strong as they thought they were, a tough lesson because that was some crazy back pain. They worked hard, that's for sure, and she triple-clicked her tongue at the memory, half amused that she could say no, not anymore, to the idea of breaking and hauling rocks. She could ditch the permit and forget about renewal. Was it a betrayal of their dream to stop doing it? She smiled while remembering Mark's physical strength, her handsome geologist husband, shirt off, swinging the maul. Mark was solid. Even when exhausted and sitting down to rest a spell he would pick up a stone, rub it on his pants leg to examine it clean under a small lens, and state with a geologist's admiration, "Goes to show ya, babe, there is no such thing as an ordinary rock."

Carola could hear the school bus rattling back down the main road on its return trip, rolling through the T-intersection with the row of mailboxes, what she called the crossroads of Dirt and Dirt since nothing was paved this far out of town. She headed back inside before its dust cloud blew over the place. She passed the papers on the patio table and picked up the rock paperweight to bring inside. If the papers blew away, that would be a kind of letting go, she told herself. She beheld the piece of ore in her palm. She loved its color, the irregularity of borders, that the precious part was organic, amoeba-like, spreading as a fluid, ink dropped into water. She heard Mark's voice in her head launching into some geology jargon, obsidian rhyolite, Precambrian granite, post-Paleozoic deformations with fault zones. Her perspective held a regard so different from his. Her own truth took on a different shape. Art and science melding together like the layers in this rock, that's the conversation they had continued for twenty-four years of marriage.

She pulled open the sliding glass door to go inside and laid the rock on the kitchen table beside cans of dog food. The name of this house was The House That Chips Built For Me. The first time she met Chips was in a little canyon on the back side of the mountain where they parked the truck before hiking into the mine. Mark and she had been hauling the Hilty Hammer and generator and fuel and gear and food out of the truck and into two wheelbarrows to bring over to the holes. Those holes were miles away over territory that could not be crossed by a vehicle. Even the wheels of the wheelbarrows could not traverse the entire distance, yet their usefulness for at least part of the way was vital relief for the hauling.

They heard the motorcycle in the mountains long before they saw it. Mark told her it must be his friend Chips, who had moved back to town after wheeling around the Midwest and California. Chips rolled up on his Harley, the noise echoing in the canyon. Carola had been surprised that Mark told Chips where to come. Their site was secret. Plenty of people wanted to know where they got blue opals, asked please could they come out there to watch, as if the mine was Knotts Berry Farm. And of course could they run around like mountain goats, get bit by snakes, distract Mark and Carola from their work, and oh yes take home some souvenirs. Those rocks were their source of income, didn't people understand that? Why would they give it away after hammering it out and carrying it on their backs.

Mark trusted Chips. She held back her admonition, biding her time. She forced herself to relax into a charm and extend a cheerful hello to Mark's annoying, boyish buddy who had a one-sided smile and seemed in need of a haircut, some dental work, and friends. Despite her initial misgivings, she yielded and they regaled her with stories that began, "Hey pal, remember when …"

Chips brought out two gifts from inside his leather jacket. A 357 Magnum and a puppy.

While Carola bonded with the puppy, the boys went to the far end of the canyon and took turns shooting cans. A burrowing owl flew out in panic. They didn't shoot it; the first explosive noises had startled the small bird. The owl flew low past Carola and she felt the air move as though her heart were transparent. She saw the owl's inquisitive eyebrows and soft feathers, brown with many dabs of white. All this she treasured. She snapped back to her tasks and wondered if Mark was going to bring Chips out to the holes to help get ore. He did. And their loads were much lighter that day. She relented and began to enjoy Chips' company.

Chips became an all or nothing kind of friend, inside their lives or not around at all. He would ride away on a spontaneous motorcycle odyssey to Mazatlan, Yellowknife,

Boston, then come back just as much in need of a haircut, hot meals, and a sense of direction, something to do to mend his heart from another broken relationship. He was the wandering boy, a rambler, lost as a doodle bug, ever returning to his mother's home in Benson, where it wouldn't take long before he argued with his mother and got his feelings hurt and roared out to their ten acres to bunk on the couch. He helped Mark put up the pre-fab metal barn that they used for a garage, then a year later when they had more cash, helped to partition the barn into rooms for a lapidary shop, storage room, and a studio. When a Neiman Marcus buyer took on her Sacahuista jewelry line they could call in the electrician, Jocko, Chips' stepfather. Flipping a switch, such sublime luxury.

The puppy grew into the dog who came in behind her now with a white muzzle and a stiff gait. She was careful to pause until his tail was all the way in before she closed the patio door. That door was getting heavier to slide these days and the dog was taking longer to get from one side of the door to the other. "You're still with me, Blue. I don't know what I'd do without you." She petted the dog for a long time, then fed him and they both took naps.

Carola dreamed about ordinary time and geologic time. She dreamed that she was in Owl Canyon, for that's the name they gave their box canyon, with its soft grassy brush, creosote and cactus. Carola heard Mark's voice, "It was the place we were excited to start from and we were always happy to get back to. It was our rest stop on the Highway to Rock Heaven." Carola laughed in her dream. "You crazy nut," she hugged him, "Rock Heaven? More like Rock Hell." And she laughed and laughed and she reached out for him again and that is when cool and absolute awakening came to her. She didn't want to be awake; she wanted to remain fuzzy and sleepy and continue the dream. To be awake was to lose him all over again.

They had carried too many loads from the holes to the truck that day, and they didn't rest long enough at the wheelbarrow stopping place. They tried too hard, pushed too hard, that's why it happened. Chips wasn't with them that bad day. They were in the middle of unloading the wheelbarrows into the truck when Mark slumped to the ground. He couldn't speak. How she got Mark into the truck must have come from adrenaline, because he was limp and heavy. "Wake up Mark, stay with me," she ordered, all while driving at the fastest speed over washboard curves, ripping through the gears, racing down the fire road. At the clinic. Mark remained unresponsive and the doctor could not bring him back from the massive stroke.

Chips took their truck back up to Owl Canyon to pick up the tools, wheelbarrows, buckets of rock, all she had abandoned. Chips held her in the mortuary parking lot where she screamed and sobbed and burned with terror and grief and pain. "I will never see him again," she cried, broken and desperate, as reality pressed on her like an immense block of stone fallen from a great height. After the funeral Jocko said that all Chips did was stay in bed facing the wall. "He's in a terrible pain of sorrow," Jocko told her with a hand on her shoulder as they stood in a gas station a week later. "And now he's gone off again on his motorcycle, destination unknown."

Everything half finished around the trailer and barn remained as though Mark evaporated. Everything that he put down on a counter remained so, keys, tools, magnifying lens, rags, half-cut, half-polished rocks. Everything that he had touched became a talisman for Carola as she moved like smoke through chaos. She would not, could not sit down in her studio, now cold and meaningless. She stopped eating anything beyond crackers. Carola drifted, getting a glass of water, drinking half, leaving the glass somewhere indoors or outdoors, and returning to lie on their bed wrapped up in Mark's sheepskin jacket in the hottest weather. The electricity got turned off because she never opened the bill. Blue would nudge her with a cold nose on her hands or feet until she got out of bed to open a can of dog food. He howled for the first 24 hours after Mark died. After that he seldom barked and the silence, night and day, blanketed the trailer. She started letting Blue sleep on the bed and sometimes when, back to back, she felt his boney spine pressing into her she dreamed it was Mark.

She awoke one day to the sounds of water running and dishes being washed. Blue was thumping his tail against the refrigerator. Chips was there. She felt woozy and annoyed. It was too bright outside. Her shoulders were cold. She sat back down on the bed and looked for her socks. Something smelled like cinnamon. She looked up. Chips was handing her a steaming mug of Mexican coffee. Her head felt full of water, a lake with opposing shores of rancor and helplessness. She reached for the mug with both hands.

Chips hauled baskets of laundry outside and Blue followed. She could hear the generator start up and the washing machine thumping in the shed. She smelled so awful that she knew she had to shower. That's what she did. Shampoo from the same bottle she and Mark had used. Lather with a bar of soap that Mark's hands had held. Her legs buckled and she put out one arm to the tile wall for support. All of a sudden the water turned from lukewarm to cold. When that happened, something settled inside her, like a lid spinning above a basket to drop into its groove atop the place of Carola and Mark.

She ate a hot meal with food Chips brought from town, and they settled into a kitchen table conversation, the kind that suspends time, goes deep and keeps everyone together. He was gone too long, he said. He was staying in town with his mother, Eden. Carola knew his mother as a grim and damaged woman with a sharp anger. Carola flinched deep inside with a feeling like discovering the outline of a knife within a made-up bed. She didn't change her facial expression. Carola had always avoided Eden. Their mutual repugnance was a woman thing of a certain type. Any other woman that her son spent time with was someone that Eden hated; and as soon as her son left the room the happy smile changed to cold dislike on Eden's face and her eyes glared with malice at the other woman. Even when Carola tried to find common ground with Eden by remarking on their mutual pioneer heritage, pointing to an old photo on the wall in Eden's home. It was a picture of the corner of Fourth and Huachuca Streets in Benson in 1890; false front stores, wooden sidewalks, horses and a buggy, women in long cotton dresses and men wearing cowboy hats. Both their families were among the first non-native settlers in southeast Arizona; their great-grandfathers were railroad men working for the Southern Pacific; their great-grandmothers were the kind of willful frontier women who didn't shirk from hard labor and who lived through losing husbands to illness, banditry and accidents. Yet Carola's bonding attempt, the similar heritage, was met by stiff aridity, evaporating faster than rain in the desert.

Was it a whole year ago that Chips died? Something brought Eden into her mind while she had been standing at the gate. She had tried to force the thought away by staring at the mountain. Eden hurt that boy. Eden put Chips in danger. Eden was the bile, the focus of Carola's anger. The nap had given her strength to face these thoughts. Carola drew out the full awareness, like picking splinters of glass from a wound.

Chips moved in and began to take care of things. He caulked the trailer roof vent. He fixed the ripped door screen. He adjusted the hot water heater. He cleaned the lapidary equipment in the barn. He gassed the truck. Her bed remained covered with newspapers, rumpled clothes, dirty bowls of gummed cereal, photo albums. Chips left that end of the trailer untouched. He remained a quiet and constant presence, never pushing. When she raged, he'd be gone for a couple days staying at his mother's until Carola forgot and softened, yielded to the worst reality, that Mark's living ended and her life went on.

After a long while her ability to taste food returned. Laughter sprung from her mouth when Chips stepped inside the trailer one winter day wearing a goofy snowboarder cap with long knitted tails on each side of his head. Their closeness grew into an organic tangle. The bed was cleared.

The House That Chips Built was their project and it was a consuming project. Carola didn't want the new house to be too big and she didn't want it ramshackle. Chips promised no road trips until the house was finished. In gratitude she gave him all Mark's tools and the Magnum 357, the second set of keys for the truck, money for gas and groceries and beer. Chips was a cabinet maker by trade and the work progressed with care. First they drew up a solid design, everything thought out and kept practical and pretty. Pour a foundation, buy used lumber, hammer the studs. His stepfather could do the electricity for cheap and get someone-who-knew-someone to do the plumbing.

Excitement stirred inside Carola, a breeze on a spark overlaid with dry grass. One afternoon she awoke a little more from her grief as she stood at the sawhorse table measuring and cutting tiles for the bathroom --- awoke because colors had returned to her vision. She had seen colors for the past year. She hadn't been blind; she knew a red traffic light, saw mold on food, saw the sky and her shoes. Instead this was a literacy of colors that returned in a sweep of artistic awakening, the speckle of browns on a tile, the pinks in the palm of her hand and backside of her fingers, the many greens in the limbs of the palo verde trees, thin line of red up the spine of a cactus, the colors of life force, her colors, her palette, her spectrum as an artist. Illumination. She began to breathe easier.

Life with Chips was not without its complications. Eden demanded his presence at home often and coming back to the ten acres, he'd be closed-in and teary. Eden was creepy with the eyes thing and Carola stayed in the truck if Chips had to stop at her house when in Benson for a Wal-Mart run or the hardware store. In Eden's presence Chips became sullen, even his posture curled inward. Every relationship meant a war game to Eden. Carola recalled one awful hot day that Eden came to the truck while Chips was in their garage with Jocko wrangling over types of electrical wiring. Eden had been laid off from her job as a medical lab technician. "Chips is mine," Eden told her, articulating each word like cactus spines. "You think you got your claws into him, but he's mine. He helps me first and that's not going to change. Jocko is not always here and I need Chips to be home, not up there as free labor building a house for you. Chips should build a house for me so I can rent it out. We need the money and you don't. You have insurance money so you're set."

That amount was much smaller than anyone would think but why should Carola tell that to Eden? Most cash that Carola gave as gift or earnings to Chips she would guess went straight to Eden. Carola knew Chips truckled to his mama, and in retrospect her own silence was tight as the valve on a propane tank.

The line was crossed for Carola, the valve over-strained so to speak, when she learned that Eden had taken to cooking crystal meth in her kitchen for easy cash and had Chips selling it. She was bored, Chips explained, and someone told her how to do it. "I just did this one thing one time so she would get off my back. I wanted to make her life easier. When I made the rounds for her, she was happy. She told me where to go each time and who to see. No complications. Not until the last sale. I got cocky. I wasn't sure if those guys were undercover."

Carola stood stock-still while he blathered this way and that, off on tangents about Eden's happiness and helping Eden just to stop her haranguing him whenever he was there, and how it was a short term one time moneymaking scheme. "She's using you and she doesn't care about you, don't you see that?" Carola called him stupid and cursed him as the argument ramped up and she said the horrible words: Get out. Don't come back.

White-muzzled Blue sat at her side now, alert to her agitation as she remembered the terrible argument. How much she wanted to purge Eden from her mind! Eden swung back up like a wicked clown target in a carnival shooting booth. Every time Carola had a visitor --- the postal carrier, old BLM friends of Mark's, the rare jewelry buyer, the UPS truck --- the same subject came up, Chips and why he shot himself. Earlier this morning it had been the propane delivery driver. She had forgotten all about the propane delivery this morning. That's what brought it back.

The driver had gone to high school with Chips and Mark. Carola admitted to the driver that she and Chips had a terrible argument about Eden. Chips stormed away, stumbled, almost falling over a small pile of rocks that had been dumped in a corner of the patio by Mark for edging a future tomato bed. Not even the ghost of Mark could stop him. When he got to the truck, Chips got the gun out from the under the seat and within seconds he turned the gun on himself, the Magnum that he had given to Mark in Owl Canyon. When she heard the shot, she was in the house. She never, never thought that Chips would commit suicide. The sight of him and all the blood was more horrible than she could explain. The propane driver told her, "I'm sorry you had to find him like that."

A mention of Eden could still crush her day. The space without Mark and Chips remained as empty. As she cried, old Blue placed his head against her knee. She made a list of everyone gone from her life, including her mother, grandmother, and the great-grandmother who had outlived three husbands, the second one killed while working as a Wells Fargo stagecoach driver during the Indian Wars, the third died from influenza. She was no closer to understanding why she remained alive; the question was unanswerable.

Maybe it had been an accident. There was no reason for him to handle the gun at that moment unless he had seen a snake by the truck. She would never know. He had shot himself and left her to find him and deal with the cleanup and tell everyone the terrible facts. And he had left her with immense anger and remorse and sadness.

Carola sat upright and breathed. She decided to create a way to rid herself of the presence of Eden in her mind. The state police had zeroed in on Eden just last week, the propane driver told her. Details blurred with his voice. From now on, every time anger about Eden came into her mind, she would take an eraser and rub it away. In time she might even forgive the egregious faults of Eden or set them in place, one stone among many in a cairn. Carola picked up a pencil on the coffee table and found a piece of paper with some empty space on it. She sketched a school board eraser, first with a light strokes to get the geometry of it just right. She cross-hatched and made a shadow, then outlines of a table top, desk, window, mountain. This would become her mental tool to take wherever she went, outside, inside, to the studio, mailbox, collecting pieces of paper that had flown out to the empty wilds, and so on. She wanted to burn this image into her mind. She would do something good for Chips. She would do something good for Mark. For their memories. She wanted to draw Owl Canyon and all its extraordinary visitors.

To go over the mountain again, she would be returning with regrets and cherished memories. They had scattered Mark's ashes in Owl Canyon. When they did she thought he'd become strata in a rock someday, eons away. Her love for Mark gave those thoughts a sanity. She wondered if the burrowing owl that they called a howdy bird was still there. She also considered that she would have to gas up the truck. Get another bag of dog food, buy oranges, fill water jugs, find her bigger sketchpad and watercolors.

She would not be breaking rock this time, or not ever again. Maybe in February she would buy amethyst at the mineral show to make silver rings, or maybe not. First, the canyon. For the present she wanted to go light, cross over the mountain, wander and draw as she absorbed its shapes and colors, details and depth. She started a to-do list and realized that to gas up the truck she'd have to go into town. To go to town, she'd be driving past Eden's house, not so close but it was indeed visible along the frontage road. Carola walked back to the living room and turned off the tv that had been on for days, weeks.

She had already answered the question, how to live in the presence of someone that you loathe. Make a mental eraser and use it every time the hateful anger rises. It might work. If it didn't, there were other solutions to be found. She would figure it out. That house, though. A perfect, splendid plant called yarrow grew wild and abundant in front of the house where Chips grew up --- the Achilles plant with little white flowers, sometimes yellow, a rambling weed found all over the west, with gorgeous leaves, the most wonderful leaves to draw --- and yarrow was the exact image she was going to hold in her memory as she drove past. How else can you get anything done?

~~ The End ~~

A BRAND NEW CADILLAC

Skinny Michael Gonzales stood near the edge of the sandy mesa behind the house where he grew up. He interlaced his hands behind his head as he looked upon wide open spaces all the way to the horizon and back again. His gaze took in the vast panorama of the southwestern landscape, gazing past the distant highway, the chaparral studded hills, the arroyos and the shimmering lake, thinking only of bridges and concrete aqueducts, earth dams, stress factors, steel, columns, girders and girls. He was thinking about college.

He turned and saw his grandfather coming toward him from the horse barn. The old man wore his customary denim shirt, work jeans and tan, beaten cowboy hat. In heeled cowboy boots, his grandfather's manner of walk was a peculiar stumble that Michael could recognize in profile from any distance. The four family dogs, two short, one medium, and one with long legs, barked and ran in happy circles around the old man.

"Michael," his grandfather's hoarse voice called out, "Is that ol' fence even worth fixing?" His grandfather never used his school nickname, Skinny M, that Michael had etched on the back window of his own pickup truck he had used for school every day.

"Si, grandpa. It's done. I just now finished." Michael picked up the post hole digger, gloves, hammer and nails and started to walk back to the barn. He caught up to his grandfather just as the old man bent one knee to the earth. "Sir! Are you all right?" Michael's heart pounded in his ears.

"Now don't get excited," the old man waved him away. "I'm just noticing something on the ground. Look here," he said after a few moments of silence. His hands scuffed around in the dirt by his knee. "Look what I found. It's some chalcedony rose."

Together they knocked the dirt off the rocks and rubbed the small white swirls of quartz on their jeans. The more they rubbed, the pinker the rock roses bloomed.

Inside the house, they put their prizes on the cluttered top of the counter by the tv, in front of the framed family photos which included a picture of Michael's father in his military uniform and his mother in her nurse's uniform. His father had died in Afghanistan. There were only three now in the house: Michael, his mother and grandfather. They were a complacent, quiet trio, a kind of family easy to overlook simply because the high drama of their lives came in small moments that were swept up like dust by the breeze of everyday living.

"That's nice," said Michael's mother as she noticed the pile of rocks near the tv. Arlene Gonzales was at the dining room table reading the newspaper, her habitual seat after coming home from working at the hospital each day. "More rocks. Where did you find those?" Her expression had all the enthusiasm of a wine maker receiving yet another clump of grapes.

"Ugly little pieces of rock, aren't they?" Grandpa commented.

Arlene relented. "Okay. They are pretty. A little dusty maybe but what's more dust when the counter already looks like the moon!"

"Mom," Michael smiled, "You can always throw them out back after I leave. Hey, we found them where the fence was down."

"I am so glad you fixed that before leaving, Michael." Arlene's expression perked up. "Between the neighbor's cattle coming smack up to the house and the chickens getting in that old car out back, it's enough to drive me crazy!" She raised her hands in mock frustration.

"I fixed up that Cadillac so's the chickens wouldn't get in it again."

"You mean you rolled up the windows?" his mother asked, deadpan.

"Wha'd you do to that old car?" Grandpa asked as he craned his neck and peered out the window at the old auto parked among the low greasewood and chaparral brush beyond the house. An empty, tireless car, without an engine, the black 1952 Cadillac four-door sedan had sat on blocks, waiting for Michael's father to come home and restore it. Over the years, the heap had been mostly ignored. But no one had ever wanted to get rid of it. Sometimes, when the subject came up, Arlene would repeat, "Oh, I don't really want to give it away or sell it. Maybe we'll do something with it someday. Just leave it where it is." Grandpa would go sit in the car for a spell every now and then. And sometimes after feeding the chickens, Arlene would be seen leaning against the front of the car, looking into the distance. Afterward, Michael noticed that she'd return to the house and play old records or turn up the radio and talk Michael and Grandpa into the idea of all three driving into town for dinner at Sonic or the cousins.

Arlene joined Grandpa at the window. She turned in surprise to Michael, "Why, that car looks like brand new. What did you do to it?"

"I washed and waxed it."

"When?"

"This morning."

"I don't understand. What's the sense of shining up a car without an engine?"

"I rolled up the windows and sprayed bug spray inside. Under the seats, too. Cleaned it up a lot." Michael was grinning. This was his going away gift to his mother and grandfather. "Come outside and see," he urged. "I aired it out after the bug spray. Come look."

They grabbed sodas from the fridge and walked out to the Cadillac.

"It's just like brand new," Grandpa smiled softly, rubbing his hands on the shiny, waxed hood.

"Please sit inside," Michael gestured grandly, opening all four of the sedan's doors.

The seats had been dusted; the dashboard wiped; and behind the front seat, a radio-cassette player had been secured with tape and wire.

"There's new batteries inside that should last until I come home at Thanksgiving and then I'll put in fresh ones for you."

Although his mother seemed pleased, as she smiled she shook her head. "That car won't be going anywhere. I don't understand why you wanted to do this."

"You will, Mom, Grandpa. Hang with me here for a moment and look at these." He pointed to the collection of cassette tapes in a box on the floor. Frank Sinatra. Hank Snow. Old Time Radio Shows. Buck Owens. Elvis. Lake Woebegone stories. Los Temerarios. Mariah Carey. The Beatles. U2. "It's just a place to sit and relax and watch the sunset."

The dogs had clambered over the open windows into the front seat and were thumping their tails on the steering wheel. They all knew a good thing when they saw it.

"I'm gonna miss you, Michael. I wish your dad were here to see you go to college." Arlene sighed. "Your dad really loved this car."

Grandpa stretched his legs out the open door. He tilted back his cowboy hat and looked at his grandson with a smile.

"Looks like when we get to missing you, Michael, we can just come out to our Cadillac and go for a ride."

"I won't be gone that long," Michael responded and winked. "Listen to this one." He selected a cassette tape, put it into the player and gestured for his grandfather to push the play button.

They sat with all the Cadillac doors wide open, the dogs in the front seat, the Gonzales Family in the back seat, all regally touring the world. The strains of Frank Sinatra's My Way wafted like invisible smoke, curling high and over and up, and catching a breeze; the melody traced a line over the piñon bushes toward the airy forever beyond the mountains. The line curled into the sky and spoke of love to the clouds which were gathering on the horizon for the sunset.

~~ The End ~~

JOSIE GOES WEST

She wore a fancy red dress that had come folded between pieces of paper inside a hide and batten trunk, trundled across the continent on varying sizes of conveyances from horse cart to ox team to stage coach and the animals of which were led by people who were survivors of wagon train rigors, bandit attack, and illness discomfort and grime, a sturdy and leathery people to whom a flounce was a passing cloud, an illusion, part of a distant tale for which there was seldom time and the color red was the tinted brushwork of the western sunset which reigned across the broad horizon at the close of daylight at the ending of every bone-wearying day spent traveling west to the lands of great promise and freely proffered opportunity, lands where their children would drink milk at every meal and dreams could come true even if a dream was so different from their dream, as hers was, to dance and act on a stage in San Francisco, singing, entertaining, applauded by the wealthy, the successful gold prospectors and society; or even if the dream came closer and much sooner in Tombstone Arizona on a Saturday night inside a low ceiling dirt floor adobe saloon where cattle drivers and stage coach drivers and whiskey drivers (as the two bartenders toasted themselves) rollicked and stamped their heavy boots upon the dirt floor to the tune of an upright piano brought out from St. Louis and on its way to California as part of the precious cargo of one particular wagon on the train, the one wagon that belonged to a brigand of singers dancers and actors, a small family troupe who shared quilts at night and songs by day and the excitement of getting ready for a show and helping Josie lace up the fancy, crease-worn and dusty red dress, a tad more grimy than decent but satin red, a true and bold red and more than ever, in that red dress she was a full part of the troupe not a child any more; even though earlier it had felt like a slavery as before the train started up for the day in the pre-sunrise hours and she wore an old grey smock and she was ordered to stir the breakfast gruel and the campfire smoke stung her eyes with the shifting wind but during the evening performance while wearing the dress and trying to remember all the lines of a song and exhilarated and nervous, a new kind of feeling developed, the sense that belonging comforted, lent pride, defiance, and the mettle to continue on toward San Francisco, despite the moments of differences between the universal Us: the entertainers, and Them: the others of the wagon train, the homestead dreamers equipped with many oxen and many sons, Norwegian and French farmers and their families, Italian, Irish, or some born slaves, some born children of indentured-for-nearly-life, some born third generation, who during the day all were heartened, encouraged, by snatches of the troupe's songs coming along the breeze up and down the rattling, bone-wearying wagon train but who could not fully understand such a dream that did not include a store or shop or farm or ranch or acres of planted corn rippling beneath the wind that precedes a rainstorm which echoed the years of toil and personal deprivation before their frontier dream would come to fruition, to harvest and to table because around the campfire these sturdy homespun pioneers had sourly mocked the girl who would wear the fancy red dress by asking, "and after you act a part in a play, what do you have when it is all finished --- look, we will have our farm and but if you pursue a fancy illusion as an actor on the stage in San Francisco, won't you only have emptiness after the audience leaves?" to which she answered with a shrug and silent resolve made more certain by a glance back toward her mother who may not have heard the question yet whose very countenance held Josie's glance for a long moment as she saw her mother, humming, with hair pinned up and shoulders set strong and hands using a rag to spot clean the red dress that used to be her own, and then holding the dress away from herself at arms length, as if holding her own daughter away from herself for a little moment as if seeing her own daughter in the distant place, as if seeing Josie moving into her own dream, her own future and with one small smile and a lift of her chin, her mother's countenance gave to Josie the strength of stubbornness and a brighter light inside the dream to carry her the remaining distance west to San Francisco.

~~ The End ~~

RENO SILVER

He knew stories about all the wandering minstrels of the west, especially those of the late 1800s and early 1900s. There was more to Reno than his relatives, dear or distant, recalled because they thought he was a junk collector. History was Reno's passion. He bought any old daguerreotype and photograph which portrayed musicians, singers and musical instruments, and he collected old song sheets and various handmade and well worn instruments (some of which no longer sustained a true note) such as guitars, lutes and ukuleles, banjos, flutes and harps, horns and harmoniums, drums and rick-a-rack noisemakers, pipes and fifes. He wrote a song once that recited a litany of the names of all the Native American tribes and their famous chiefs; it was a response to the popular song I've Been Everywhere and it was a hit.

Reno collected and could recall old stories and old ballads about the railroads and the lands and the waters and the dreams; the western marshals who dead-eyed the endless procession of gunslingers and horse thieves, rapers and bandits, weaving in the stories of Chinese-American cowboys and Polish-American cowgirls; Midwest Scandinavian immigrants; and the doe-eyed orphans who could only guess at their ancestry. Their stories were sagas of falling in love, daring to enter the frontier, birth and death and work and dust; friendship and sorrow and meals on the table; mean bosses and straw bosses; hotels and telegraphs; Sweet Betsey From Pike; church bells and sad sights, weddings and bar fights; and friendships and courtships and daybreak from the open flaps of a tent; and stakes and claims and horses and oxen and chickens and foxes and sheep, roadrunners and ptarmigan and diamondbacks and snowbirds; itinerant singers and a piano in a lonely dusty railroad dispatch office; indian brown babies, pink Caucasian babies; the spectacle of traveling medicine shows and magic shows; the skin on the knuckles of a dying prospector; the words and voice of a Negress of royal ancestry from New Orleans; weaving in folklore about steeping yarrow tea; and about seeing the buffalo for the first time and the deepest snow and overflowed river and the year the house burned down. Collecting pieces of stories about people whose names are scarcely remembered by their relatives four, six, nine generations down the line. How much time sprints in a quick pace dripping moments, only moments that linger without end --- the moments of history, the moments of I memory: the birth of a baby, the sight of an eagle, catching a bouquet, a fly-ball, hearing the whisper of a ghost-spirit, the realization of death.

And some of this he sang one early morning at the beginning of the year, sliding from one tune to another in a reverie of history-bliss, humming the patches of verses not rising quickly enough from the tucked away parts of the brain.

With great skill Reno fingered the strings of a small brown guitar, a 1947 Martin D-28, stroking arpeggios across the fret hole, listening to the resonance of each string beside the next. He was a rangey-gaunt man, wearing a rumpled dark jacket and a plain shirt with a string tie that had a sizeable chunk of turquoise. His hair was long and grey. He was seated in the front passenger seat of an older model station wagon, parked in front of a pawn shop. Starlight had gone from the sky and sunrise was eminent. As he shifted to a more comfortable position on the front seat, his feet kicked aside various soda cups, discarded food wrappers and an empty whiskey bottle. Straight ahead through the windshield the sunrise colored the sky above the buildings, irradiating the wet dewfall on the city street.

"This is a pretty good guitar you want to sell me, Serena," he slurred a little with fatigue as he spoke to a woman who was laying down across the back seat. Reno studied her profile, the line of her forehead, her nose, jawline. Exotic heavy eyelids, a Cajun nose, however, her bones seemed prominent more than ever, her color was pallid. She seemed to breathe in little puffs, without much strength in her body. "I'd say we could have a deal. Sure am glad you stopped by after the show. Honey, it's been too long. Too damn long between sunrises."

"Is that what this is called? A sunrise?" she responded with a sullen tone. "Maybe I've been looking to the right and left too long. I've forgotten how to look up."

"Serena, you a sourpuss. C'mon hon." He strummed softly. "Do you remember the song about the cowboy and the nurse who meet in a cafe for coffee, and they're both married?"

She smiled, "But not to each other. Old Friends And Old Lovers. That was one of the best we ever wrote." She sang, "Old friends and old lovers, caught between others trying to keep them apart. They meet sometimes for coffee and remember all they can speak of without breaking their hearts." She fell silent for a while. "Do us a favor and don't play that one anywhere. It will make me laugh and you cry or else me cry and you laugh and Reno there's nothing worse than to hear you blow your nose near a microphone." With the heavy effort of one foot Serena pulled down on the handle and shoved open the car door. It creaked slowly open across the sidewalk and stayed open; the street was empty of traffic; the morning air was cool and sobering in its urban morning manner; and she made no motion to leave the car.

The sun's rays slipped between skyscrapers and shone on the San Angelo street sign, Second Avenue and River Street. The curb in front of the One & Only Pawn Shop was grey and splotchy. Second Avenue was lined with warehouses and old hotels and bars with ugly facades. On that street everything looked eaten into by acerbic microbes from air pollution, the grease of too many fingerprints and the thousands of occasional passersby who hunkered, leaned, pissed and rested against the square stone corners, the quoins, on some of the buildings.

"We're known each other for a long time, Reno."

"Through four of my wives. Lord, how they come and go," Reno scratched his beard.

Serena moved her velvet eyes then followed with her head. "I got to talk to you about something. All we know about each other any more, and this is truth because time and distance have happened to both of us," she intoned only a slight pause, "Is that you and I come down pretty quick to the fundamental of dirt honest with each other. You know that and I know that. And we are probably too damn forthright to live comfortable for very long with other people, I guess. Enough of that. Look, Reno, I'll come right out with why I went and found you. I need to talk to you straight about something. I am sick. I got cancer bad and there's things to be dealt with. And furthermore," she patted his arm as she sat up, "There's no one else I can enjoy getting roaring drunk with except you."

Reno sat very still.

Serena started to get out of the car, "I've got peach brandy put up. It's in the back room. Come inside. There's some news that I got this week that concerns the both of us and I need to talk with you about it. Book it. Come on inside now."

Serena unlocked the roll down security grill on the One & Only and Reno lifted it up for her while holding the Martin between his knees. The grill's rumbling clang echoed along the empty street. The sun was coming on strong; this was only the first grill absorbed by buildings, sidewalks and street. Other would soon follow. Until then cocooned in blankets, the rest of the world remained on the other side of somewhere, at a quiet place, a softer place, far away from downtown. Cocooned far away from parking garages and garbage odors, asphalt, metal grilled doors, graffiti and stained sidewalks.

Inside the pawn shop, Serena re-locked the doors. "Take a last look around 'cause I sold the shop," she announced with an arms-wide flourish. "The escrow is about finished. It'll go to the end of next week. I tell you, Reno, taking the inventory just about wore me out."

Reno glanced around the room, taking in counters piled with radios and stereos, crystal wedding goblets, silver platters, hanging rows of electric guitars and chunky accordions. Inside the glass cases, shiny metal watches, guns, rings and turquoise necklaces laid flat on velvet like the fallen-out pages of a forgotten book. Everything inside the shop held the climate of the night, the weather of the attic, the season of the closet. At the cashier's thick, wired glass window, a television set remained turned on; and, without sound, a talk show host interviewed two wrestlers who threatened each other with fist and facial gestures. Their fleshy physiques were interrupted by a commercial which presented an advertising-generic vista of green mountain landscape and scrolling song titles.

Serena led him into the rooms behind the cashier cubby. Inside the first there was a desk and piles of instrument cases, and inside the farthest back room there was a bed and kitchenette. Against the wall were open cardboard boxes filled with books and bric-a-brac. Some items were marked with small stickers that said 25 cents, 50 cents.

"Serena, are you still going to the yard sales?" He was unable yet to reply to her words about cancer. Maybe he heard her wrong.

She replied with clarity, "Not any more. I told you, I sold this place. Hey, those yard sales were fun. If I saw something and I got that old feeling that it was gonna sell, yes sir, I loved when that feeling came into me, a psychic tingle so to speak. Comes from my genes. Here," she poured two glasses of a thick orange liquid from a dusty bottle. "Make a toast, Reno."

"To your psychic mother?"

"Okay but keep going."

"To old friends and old lovers?"

"Now that's a brandy toast." She lifted her glass to touch his. "To old friends and old lovers. Oh my, I got to rest a little here on the bed. Sit on this chair, pull it over. Do you really want that guitar, Reno? It's yours. I give it to you."

Taking a sip from his glass, Reno grimaced. "Whoo, what a kicker. What did you put in this?"

"I made myself it with vodka and peaches," she boasted.

"Oh, Lawd, Serena. It's awful. No, I'm joking." He shook his head, "I guess it'd be good on ice cream."

"You liked me with ice cream," she flirted. "Makes me think of Lover Boy And Me. Play that one, would you honey? I haven't sang Lover Boy And Me in a long time. It was a good song too and no one, no one, wanted to record it. Why is that? Why does the world work like that? Roll of the dice I guess."

"Who knows honeybun. The fun was in the making." He brought the chair closer to the bed and brought up the guitar to strum.

"Oh, that tune takes me back. You know, Reno, a person reaches for a match to light a cigarette and suddenly ten, twenty years have gone by. Why does time move like that, in surprises like lightning? Lover Boy. Do you remember," she reached under the bed, "do you remember that hot summer night when you put a scoop of vanilla on my bellybutton?" Serena tugged out a suitcase from beneath the cot. "Remember how sticky we got?"

"Like butterscotch," Reno said in a low voice that seemed to swirl the air between them. Reaching out, he touched her fingers lightly and pulled her hand away from the suitcase to his knee. He drew his fingers along the inside surface of her arm to the elbow, against the smooth skin past the hollow of her elbow, to the inside of her arm and up to the crease beneath her shoulder. "We had something good, didn't we, Serena?"

She closed her eyes and did not speak for a moment.

He traced his fingers along her shoulders and neck and cheek. He leaned into her hair. Then stopped and said softly, "Mercy, woman you are becoming just bones."

Then Serena held his hands lightly. "Don't be concerned about that. When you get old, the skin gets thinner. There's another matter and it is serious."

" What is it, beauty queen, what's bothering you?"

"Cancer."

As he wiped the tears from Serena's cheeks he could not hold back his own sob.

She brought herself to calm before he did. "Be still, Reno, my good man, my one man. Sit up now. I need to tell you something important."

"It's been the longest time since I seen you girl," he lapsed into an accent and phrasings he hadn't used for years. "I been gone too long, too long. Got to be more'n a year when I came to get that mandolin. Where is this in you, girl? What can we do bout it?"

"Well, you got your business and I got mine, Reno, and there's nothing different about that. That's what always kept us apart. And life is good for you now because you got hit songs under your belt. But keep your health, Reno, keep your health because when that goes, nothin' brings it back."

"You been to a real good doctor?"

"I been to four doctors, two were real good and I trusted them, and they all talk to other doctors who say the same thing." She chuckled drily, "Each one charged me more than the one before. Someone put a whammy on me and I don't have the strength to fight back. Charms and herbs ain't gonna work this time no-neither. Hey, Reno," she swerved on the subject. "I really liked going to hear you play your music tonight. It brought back the good memories. Worth the price of the ticket I had to pay."

Reno shook his head, "Next time tell me first, hon, and I'll send tickets for you. You don't never need to pay to see my shows."

"Thank you but I don't think there'll be another time."

"Serena, I don't mean to hurt your feelings but right now my mind is on what you told me about your being sick and I think we should find a fifth doctor."

She admitted, "The guitar was just to get you here, okay, and you really like that guitar, don't you?"

"I do very much. Wait until Charley Bellstone hears the sound in this beauty. You know how he likes good sounding instruments. Hear me now, I said we should find a fifth doctor."

"Say hello to Charley for me. We all go back a long ways, don't we? My dear Reno, my sweet man, I can't waste time with chit-chat. I'm starting to fade out. I'm tired but I need to tell you about news I got for you and it's not about me being sick, although that pinches on it. Pull out this here suitcase all the way from under the bed and open it up for me."

An unusual design marked the top of the old style leather suitcase, broad lines tooled into the leather, a box made of arrows. He placed the suitcase on a chair close to the bed and paused to trace the design with his finger, gathering his feelings until a shuddering sign came from him and he snapped the locks to open.

Serena searched through disheveled contents of scarves and beribboned mementos, trinkets and antique medallions, souvenir figurines and coins and photos and greeting cards, feathers and swizzle sticks. A small wooden box was the object of her search.

"This stuff came to me from my mother and over the years I threw more things in here to save."

The wooden box and a Christmas card were bound together by a rubber band. Inside the card was a portrait photo of an infant. She held it out to Reno. His face remained without expression until she said, "I got a phone call this week from the baby I gave up for adoption twenty-two years ago. Your baby."

The sound of traffic on the street outside became audible. Active daylight entered the pawn shop without knocking and spilled into the back room, warming and lighting the ticketed objects, exciting the dust which danced in the angled shafts of the light. The sunshine diminished the gray flickering of the television where a choir with long blue robes and white collars sang and swayed soundlessly, endlessly. The first back room was full of light that pressed forward through the open door and crossed the table and the bed. Daytime had come on strong. It would hold on for a long span of hours and nothing would change it. Daytime was stronger than anyone.

"Serena, twenty years."

"Twenty-two years."

He blew a sigh, "That was long ago. We were so messed up, hon, wild and selfish. Maybe stupid, too."

"We were crazy-stupid, Reno. Hopping from one place to another. Drinking and fighting and what did we know about life? All I wanted to do was sing and I didn't want a baby to hold me back. You too. You didn't need to know anything more than the fact that I took care of it. You were with that Louise from Massachusetts then she dragged you to LA. She didn't want you to have any contact with me."

"She didn't understand me."

"No?"

"Not like you. That's why we broke up after Barbara Rose was born."

"Oh, Reno, it's all long ago. You and your life, me and mine. Not to say now if there is a right or wrong to us giving up a baby, right or wrong, up or down, it was done. I cried a lot back then and then I moved forward somehow. Someone else has raised our boy and he is grown up now. He's a man and he has his own life. He wants to meet me and maybe he will let me be in his life a little, maybe you too. For what I have left, a year, because I'm done with chemo and the stem cell cannot happen, so it's in the bad stages. I don't know how it will go when he gets here, I wish I wasn't sick when he does. When he comes it may be too complicated, it may go smooth, it may be wonderful."

She sat up in bed and kept her gaze soft and direct into Reno's eyes, "Being pregnant came as a complete shock to me back then and I was so stunned and I was so sure that I did not want a baby. He was adopted. That's fact one. He has been gone from us. That's fact two. You were in LA and loving someone else. Why couldn't I have done it different? Another fact, I could not do it different, wish I could have but facts is facts. He was always in my thoughts, always, every day, and I didn't expect that part of it and besides what could you do about it? What could you do? There was nothing more. I could do nothing but regret and move forward. Am I making sense?"

Reno nodded. They were holding hands.

"I had dreams saying good-bye to that child. I had dreams saying hello. I had dreams of being lost in a strange city with twisty-turn streets. Back then I was terrified of having a baby and not taking care of the baby right. Understand? What else could I do? Adoption seemed sensible. What's done is done."

Reno remained very quiet and at last he murmured, "If we had stayed together we …"

"Maybe. Yes, maybe we could have raised him. We could have ended up hating each other. He would have been a messed up kid. From what I know now he's turned out to be a good kid. Face it, you have a different life now, Reno, think about yourself back then. You been walking down your own life's road."

"Serena, I wish, I won't, I can't." His mouth would not work right with what his heart and brain wanted him to say.

"Hush and listen. We have to rise up and think clearly and that's always been a big bother for both of us, right? Am I right? I knew I'd get you to smile. Listen to me. This is what happened, Reno. This here is the straight facts. The woman just died and the man died the past year and the boy went through their papers and he found my name and he got the phone number since I'm still living in the same state and because I have a business."

"That sounds simple."

"Sometimes it goes that way. The most complicated things end up very simple."

"Who were they?"

"Indians from Phoenix."

"Indians adopted our baby? Where did he grow up? India?"

"Native Americans. Indigenous. They were both lawyers. She taught at a law school. Apparently he worked a lot in Washington, D.C. I suppose they have to, you know, that's where the battles are fought now. All I remember is I didn't care about their nationality or their religion. I thought they were rich. They were educated. When they came to take the baby, they were kind people. They said they were also going to visit the Cherokee Nation Museum. Why I remember that, I didn't understand until now. You know, it stuck in my mind over all these years and maybe because to me it meant that they cared about being connected together and that my baby would be a part of something bigger than all of us. I only saw them in the hospital for fifteen minutes. Or maybe an hour. Or maybe just moments. They came, smiled at me, kissed my baby boy and took him away. All three of them slipped out of my life."

Reno recovered enough to clear his voice and ask, "Is he coming here?"

"Sooner or later. To meet us."

"Serena, are you sure it's him?"

"It's him, Reno."

"Over the years hon' I did think now and then about our baby so I don't want you to feel I never did. But one thing for sure I never talked to anyone about it. We were like it never happened. That's my private sin, I guess, 'cause I never thought I'd have to look at the whole situation again until Judgment Day. No, I just never thought I'd have to look at it ever. That's the way it set with me. I guess that's where I'm a hypocrite, a sinner and a beggar for forgiveness. I'm always too busy with so-called important business. My own self seems to be a big empty storeroom I fill up with distractions."

"There's nothing to forgive. Don't go on about that. What's done is done. Now listen. He's coming here." She wobbled with weakness, "I'm not feeling good right now, Reno." She laid back on the bed, silent while they held hands and then she repeated, "He wants to meet us."

"Serena, I am too old. I got all kinds of commitments and contracts and drawbacks and faults and crankiness and hell, hon', I never was cut out to be a daddy. Besides, he could be all grown up like he don't need a daddy. Makes me think what does he really want?"

She shook her head, "You talk yourself down. You took care of Barbara Rose."

"She most took care of herself. She was only a child for a little while and then she became a teenager right under my nose and she started acting like she was made of barbed wire. I was on the road a lot, touring. Charley's wife kept her close with their brood. Then she came with me on the road and worked the shows, like everyone else on the crew, singing and hauling and re- stringing instruments and washing jeans in motel bathtubs."

"I realize that, Reno. This is important. He is coming but not right away. I may not get to see him because of the cancer. I didn't tell him I was sick. I arranged to sell the shop last month when the doctors drew their final conclusion after my third round of chemo and radiation. That's why you have got to take charge here." She paused because Reno was crying. "Stop and blow your nose. I cannot take that noise! Blow again. I need you clear headed while we talk this business all the way through. I am laying it all out. At first the doctor thought it was my gall bladder but then they found a tumor in my pancreas and everywhere else. Like I got some hard, set up concrete inside. Look at the pills I have to take. And they don't even work."

She reached under the bed again and brought out a shoebox filled with orange plastic medicine bottles. Counting out fourteen pills, she swallowed them with small sips of brandy from her glass that was nearly as full as when it was first poured. "They're poisoning me, Reno." Her voice began to break, "I can't eat anything and I'm scared all the time."

He got her a glass of water and helped her to lie back on the bed. He sat beside her, stroking her hand. "What can I do?"

"If only Mama were alive," Serena told him, "She would know what herbs to mix, a charm to set. Oh, I take that back. Her charms never worked too well on the family."

Reno spoke softly, "Tell me our boy's name."

"Harry."

"A Jewish name?"

"It's English, too. I don't know, Reno. Shake loose some of those set ideas you've got. I didn't give him a name, they did. Don't you like it? I do. I think my mama would have liked the name Harry. She would say that Harry is a musical name, like chimes."

"When is the boy coming?"

"He said not right away. He's not a boy, Reno. He is a young man, twenty-two years old. This suitcase, I want you to take it and give it to him." She motioned toward the lid, "Look, remember the box of arrows?"

His fingers traced the design. "That was our mark. We'd draw it on the sand at the lake, and we put it on all our amplifiers and cases. Your mama made that charm," Reno reminded her.

"You think it worked?" Serena wondered, silent for a long moment. "Here I am at the end of my life and we are meeting together."

"Don't say end."

"It is, Reno. Please don't wipe away my chance to leave me with some dignity and be able to say some proper good-byes and get loose ends tied up."

"You always were about a pint over the top with business."

"I had to be. Always did. Mama and Raynie were floaters. Dreamers. Look at what happened to Raynie when she disappeared. My sister didn't take to Texas. She gets depressed and just floats away and nobody every hears from her again. Open that up and look inside there," she drew herself back to the matter at hand. "Inside this case are pictures of my family and old things that have been handed down, little things passed on through the family. This all has to go to Harry. But not this little thing, however, I almost forgot about it until the other day I was doing the inventory for escrow and found the suitcase again. I had that saved out for you. There's something inside the velvet pouch that is very special. See, that's for you. You can decide whether or not he should have it when you are ready to give it up. My mother called it the singing sphere. Hold it up to your ear and you can hear the angels singing."

Reno held the ball to his ear for a long moment. "You're telling stories, Serena," he teased.

"My honeybun, I am leaving you three things, a grown-up baby who is coming to meet you, a Martin guitar and a charm to make music. Be content," she smiled.

"Serena, let's get you to another doctor."

"No, Reno. I already been to four and they been to fourteen experts and I have waited a long time in three different hospitals and now I know and I feel that my end is coming. I am winding down, Reno. I don't like it, but that's the way the old road goes up and down and over hills and curves around."

"You remember those lines."

"We sang that song together first time we were on the Opry."

"Do you regret getting out of singing?"

"I never stopped, Reno. The audiences just got smaller. Not like you with your concert audience of thousands. Look, we both fell in love with other people so life went around a corner."

Reno shook the ball, "What is this supposed to do? It looks like a Christmas tree ornament."

"No, don't be harsh with it. Treat it with care. It's a singing sphere, the real thing. My mother was a good conjurer for other people. This is what you do. When you are all alone, shake the ball and hold it to your ear. My mother was a real good at making a quitch. Just a quiet woman who knew how to read a fortune, make poultices and herb bags and charms. All kinds of charms, for love and luck and money. Okay some were stinky," she laughed softly. "You know I'll never understand why she couldn't conjure up a charm to make the family rich. No, don't hold it to your ear for too long or you'll go to sleep. Shake it somewhere when you're all alone. It'll help you make a special song. Find out if Harry sings."

"You'll be here when he comes."

"No, Reno. I won't."

"Yes you will."

"I know what I know. You find out if maybe he sings, maybe he's musical. I hope so. Then you can give this to Harry when it's your time."

"I can't believe you're saying this. Where did your mom get this thing?"

"In trade from a French Moroccan who wanted a love charm instead. Or maybe he was Turkish. He bought it in an antique shop in Naples Italy, a little dusty place."

"Where the door sticks."

"And a bell rings when you open it."

"And there are not too many lights on inside."

"And the room is full of magic."

"The best place to find and it's not on any maps!"

"My guess is before that it may have come from Ethiopia, maybe across the Sahara, the Gobi, maybe Egypt. See, there's a name on the bottom. Looks like Nectarebo."

She closed her eyes. Weariness pressed upon her and she lay still and her chest rose and fell quickly from a little bit of fever. Reno worried she had fallen asleep until she opened her eyes briefly. "I get tired. Then it passes. Sorry. I'll say it all and then I have to rest. Everything else in the suitcase, just give it to Harry when he comes. When he don't find me, he'll look for you."

"You didn't tell him you were sick?"

"No, I didn't. Promise me he'll get it. Because this suitcase is all I have of the Joyeaux family things and what little I can pass on. What else can we do for him to make up for the stupid mistakes of our lives? It scares me, Reno, that he gets in touch just before I die. Sometimes over the years I wondered almost every day what would I say to him if we ever met, and when I heard his voice on the phone, I could hardly speak loud enough for him to hear."

Reno made the promises. He wiped the tears. He arranged an faded patchwork quilt embroidered with flowers over her frail body and the room held a stillness despite the rattle of traffic outside. Creases set deep across his forehead. He picked up the small brown guitar, and he sang Serena to sleep with soft ballads and hymns. His Eye Is On The Sparrow.

Time passed, tick tock and endless. Time stretched beyond 32 bars, beyond six weeks, beyond the hospice bedside retelling of chapters of lives. They would whisper each story with a phrase 'when we lived together' and 'once when we were apart,' Reno and Serena, retelling the times spent wandering over the horizon. Seven weeks later Serena Joyeaux died in the San Angelo hospice with Reno at her side.

Serena had sold the One & Only Pawn Shop to pay her medical bills and there was little left, very little. Reno paid those remaining bills and he arranged for burial service and plot. At the hospice he was given her quilt, the suitcase and a small box of her personal belongings, containing mostly medicinal supplies, a toothbrush, underwear, a jar of face cream. Even before she passed he had searched through the suitcase, looking for Harry's address, the adoption parents' address, or at least the envelope that belonged to the Christmas card with the infant photo. He could not find an address anywhere; he did not have a last name for Harry. The card was signed, "We will be thankful to you all our lives" and there was no name.

He turned to Charley Bellstone, his longtime business partner, friend, and side man for help locating his son. He brought up the subject a week after the funeral. They were in a dressing room in a small casino waiting to go onstage. There was a technical problem with the lights and it caused a lengthy delay.

"I knew something was eatin' at you, Reno," Charley admitted. "You haven't been yourself. But I thought it was all grief from Serena's passing. You sure you want to talk about this right before we go on?"

Reno nodded an affirmation, "I've got to get it out. I have this feeling that I've forgotten to do something important and it's gonna catch up to me."

Charley was a big man, with sloped shoulders and a kind face. "That is a kind of haunt."

"I made a promise. I've got to do something about finding this boy."

"Time and destiny work together," Charley responded, watching the hallway. "If he found Serena, she must have told him who was his daddy"

"I can't be certain of that. Why hasn't he found me before this? Why can't I find him?"

"Here's an idea, Reno. How about people who will search for lost relatives. Let's get Barbara Rose and Russell to arrange for one of those searchers. You got the money now to do that. You told her yet?"

Reno shook his head. "No amount of money is going to guarantee what he's going to say to me when we meet."

"Didn't Serena tell you he was raised by good people? Think with your heart, not your head on this one, Reno. Don't make more out of this than has happened. Take the right steps but take them slow."

"I'm getting a second chance and I want to do something with it. I want to show you something Serena gave me." He opened Serena's suitcase and revealed its contents.

Charley held the silver ball in his hand and shook it. "I like this sound. Maybe we can amplify it, like a tinkley kind of marimba."

"No, don't mess with it. It's for him, for Harry."

"That his name? Is he a musician? You don't know? Where did Serena get this thing?" Charley asked, swinging the ball back and forth on its chain. Reno told him.

"So presto-magico this is an instant song maker? Do we get rich now or later?" Charley asked but didn't wait for an answer. "Don't show it to my Russell or he will figure a way to take it apart and hook it up into his computer. I ought to be happy he handles the road so well using his spreadsheets and such."

"Leave him be. If that's what Russell does well in life, more power to him. Somebody's got to add up the numbers. Me, I always gravitate toward the mysterious things. They have a certain character, that's all. Charley, why am I hesitating. I am being so obstinate. I'm excited to find him and I'm wary of finding him." Reno took the sphere from Charley and put it on the dressing table.

Charley became very serious. "How do you know that Serena told you the truth?"

"She did."

"Reno, that family of hers was nutty. Truth was a fluid substance for them. Remember Mama Joyeaux with her potions and Serena's sister Raynie, the one who never came out of the bayou?"

"Couldn't find Raynie when I buried Serena. They never had any phone and when I called the sheriff down there in the parish they lived in, well, the deputy told me that no one was living on their land anymore and that he thought someone said that Raynie took off with a carnie years ago. Charley, truth is that I knew Serena got pregnant by me and I knew that she gave the baby up for adoption. I never did do nothing about it. It was not a big matter to me at the time; that's how young and stupid I was. I thought it was something she could handle and she did take care of it and that was the end of it. Then when I took in Barbara Rose years later after my brother and his wife died in the car crash, well, I did think about Serena's baby but I still didn't do anything about it. Figured he had a life all arranged and I would just mess it up. You remember, with Barbara Rose that I didn't really know what I was doing, taking on the support of a kid eleven years old."

"Barbara Rose raised herself. That's what everybody says."

"You and Lynn, you two did most of it. I am grateful."

"We were lucky that she was a good kid. She is a blessing in all our lives. And now she gives us orders. Maybe you shouldn't have put her in the business because she sure likes to order us around, just like Russell. I swear they both crack the whip snap-snap and somehow we still love 'em to death."

"Yeah, it worked out all for the good."

"On the other hand, how do you know this boy is yours? Now don't be insulted. When this boy does show up, how do you know if he's aiming to latch onto you for money reasons? Just playing devil's advocate, you understand."

"Serena thought he had a good life. And we both know how money is only green colored paper." Reno dangled the ball in the air, "Magic ball tells me we're looking old. You got jowls and wrinkles just like me and paranoia too." He heaved a sigh, "When he comes I want to have a feeling that we will work it out and it will all be good."

Charley shrugged. After a moment he reached for the little ball, rubbed it thoughtfully and handed it back to Reno. "What is that ball worth among antique collectors?" he asked.

Reno frowned, "I think I'm hearing something out there, Charley, they might be ready for us. Charley, it's a curio. Came out of her box of curios and ephemera, memories and little precious worn out things, ribbons and postcards and glass bead necklaces, feathers and old fountain pens and bits of pretty wrapping paper, old letters, empty envelopes, scraps of song. I did some reading about these balls. There was a minstrel in the 1800s reputedly had one."

"A magician who pulled it out of a hat!" Charley laughed. He turned at the sharp knock on the dressing room door.

Russell stood in the open doorway. "Time. Dad, Reno, let's go right now, I mean right now. You got to hustle." He was a young fellow with short hair and earrings. "You had the speaker turned off. Barbara Rose and the rest of them are waiting onstage, already warmed up the crowd. They finally got the lights fixed."

Reno stood up and as an afterthought asked in a low voice, "Hey Charley I don't think it's going to be about the money with him. You got money bothering you right now? You're doing all right by me, aren't you?"

"Never said I was unhappy, did I?" Charley picked up his electric bass and moved toward the doorway. Russell nodded his head at his father and angled it toward Reno in a silent communication. Charley got the point. "Russell here thinks you should give me credit on some songs, Reno. As co-writer and the rest of it."

"When you write them, I will." Reno's replied tightly, possessively. "You'll get credit when it comes."

Russell remained silent. His father looked away.

Reno continued, "Meantime, let's make this crowd jump."

"Come on, come on, hurry it up and let's get out there," Russell waved them into the hallway, "Can't you two hear that roaring crowd?" He indicated with his thumb. "They're happy for you."

Going out the doorway, Reno turned back to Charley and grasped his arm. As usual before a show he was scared and excited and tense, all the complexities of jitters, and with a tone of apology, he took back his harsh words, "I flew off half-cocked, Charley. That's my old ways. My bygone ways. Let's do your two songs Battered and Thumpin' Family Heart at the top of the second set, Charley. I'll introduce you and do a lead up."

Russell said in an undertone to his father as he passed, "Get him to put it on his next album."

"I heard that, Russell. It can go on the live album."

"Hey, what's got into you? I like it."

Charley put a hand on Reno's back. "We'll find this Harry for you. It can be done. We'll help."

They walked the long white hall with half-grins, settling their insides and lifting themselves and repeating silently the first lines of the first song as they went up the short stairs and across the side stage and stepped cautiously among floor cords, tech crew and equipment into where the air fluttered and battered, lifted and soared with its enormous barrage of cracking applause and welcome cheers and fans yelling their love.

~~ The End ~

SHEILA'S ONLY-THE-LONELY BUTTE

  My sister left a note on the bedside table addressed to The Family. I read aloud, "This is the worst day of my life. I am too miserable to go on." The words sunk into my heart. My head held onto a repeating thought, 'What made this day worse than any other day in Sheila's life?' The truth was, she didn't have many good days. Four hours max, then she'd sink again. I could hold with her for an evening, or for coffee or breakfast or a ride to check the fences on the ranch. Four hours max, then she'd sink again. We'd ride along the fences on the ranch and by the time we got through currying and be ready to head back to town, he would come outside and she'd couldn't get around him, and one remark led to another and there it went, her cynical why-bother would take hold again. In the car she'd say I'm fine, I'm fine, and there would be a dullness in her face, the light had gone out.

  Sheila had done pills before, twice, and this time it worked all the way through and we were here too late. She wore her pain like the halo of a sad song. We had worked so hard at what to do to make it better for her, Mimi and me, we worked so hard and we failed. We thought we could help push away what hurt so bad.

I touched Sheila when we all showed up and I knew she was gone. Outside her bedroom window, her horse was lying on the ground in the corral. He got up suddenly, all twenty hands tall, polished bronze with a dark mane and eyes that saw us and knew everything. Old Sparta saw everything, if you were brave enough to tell him the truth and that was easy when you loved a horse. Sheila loved Old Sparta. The dogs were howling with grief.

I turned and regarded my father very clear and judgmental because he had killed her as sure as putting pills inside her mouth. Everything he did was the cause of Sheila dying. His pinched face resembled the beady eyes and small mouth of a rodent. He knew that I knew when I read the third and last sentence of the note. "He is doing it to Mimi."

Our little sister.

A rage took hold of me to kill him. I shoved hard and he launched backward against the wall of Sheila's old bedroom, right up against her black Roy Orbison poster. Bucky grabbed my arms and held them across my chest and dragged me out of the bedroom. "Sister, you go calm down," he thundered.

"He won't stop. He had to do it to Mimi too," I rasped. The fight was gone from me as fast as it had come. Suddenly I felt like a piece of paper, no strength, blank and empty. I needed Sheila. Come back. No, she's gone forever. I kept trying to drill it into Bucky, "He did it to her," yet he was as unresponsive and confused as ever. "I want to bring her back too," he sobbed.

In the hall I slid to the floor and curled up in a misery of freezing and fever. There was a tray of Anaheim chiles on the hall table, sorted for roasting. Sheila had picked them in her vegetable garden. I took one in my hand and held its smoothness against my cheek, something she had touched, the perfection of its greenness, the tip, the stem, the long triangular beauty of a green chile, could smell its rawness. I knew. My brother knew. Mom knew. My little sister knew.

"The worst day of her life," I screamed and my voice had no strength; the words came out as dry as caleche.

Bucky pulled me up and made me go sit in the kitchen. He swung shut the door to the hall and stood over me. "Are you crazy? He'll shoot us all."

"Not this time. We have to call the sheriff this time. There's no hiding now. He can't hide now. I'll testify."

"Don't do that. We'll lose everything."

Everything? Six horses and eight head of cattle, a garden and so much land that it had become a family burden for everyone to chip in on the property taxes year after year?

We both heard Mom's car pull in at full speed and slam to a stop. I gave my brother The Look. We were terrified like we had done something wrong. It didn't make sense but that was the feeling. Mom wouldn't ever talk about anything that was real. Sometimes we kids called her Living In The Bubble, a nickname that had become repulsive now. She lived in a bubble of her own making. That's how she coped. You could talk to her about what's for dinner, but don't try to talk about anything else. She liked to live in town and she worked in a dress shop on the plaza. We could stay with her in the apartment any time, and we did, all through high school. The horses drew us back. The trick was never to come alone and to saddle-up so fast that he couldn't corner you. Always best to bring someone with. We would blast out of there before he could get a feel in. I remember Sheila's horse kicked him once. That was a day of glory.

Mom would come out on holidays like Thanksgiving and 4th of July and make a big deal of a group hike to the top of Lone Butte with us girls and Bucky and afterward serving a big meal with Dad seated at the table, a meal that she had cooked in the condo and transported out to the ranch in the trunk of her car, every bit of it, even the plates and silverware, which sometimes went back to town dirty in a cardboard box because she had reached her limit and needed to blast out of there. You couldn't say any one word beyond what was allowed. You had to be really careful, no bursting-bubble remarks allowed, no certain tone of voice allowed, no sneering looks, because she would run away instead of replying with plain common sense. Mom was like enchiladas without chile, a horse without a mane, a fence without a gate. Something essential was missing. As I said, Living In A Bubble.

You see, he tried it once on me. He said, it's our secret, don't tell anyone or you'll get beat. I was a different personality. I went right away to tell my mother. When she retorted that I always was trying to make trouble, I told my teacher the next day. She came out to the house and my parents sat at the kitchen table with her and declared that I was a Big Liar and argued a case of sibling rivalry. It was around the same time that they couldn't afford the psychiatrist anymore for Sheila that my mom moved to town. Those who wanted to get out of there went with her, more or less. We came back every day to care for the horses and sometimes stayed the weekend. We rode and walked across the land, down into arroyos, up the butte, around the cattle guards and through the barbed wire gates onto the back sides of other ranches, exploring, breathing, finding peace to put in our pockets like smiles. The land gave us peace.

Sheila's letter was still in my hand. While Bucky opened the outside kitchen door for Mom I put my hands under the table, folded the letter and stuck it down into my jeans pocket, very carefully and quickly somehow despite that my whole self was shaking in sub-zero desolation. How dare Sheila leave me alone to deal. It wasn't happening that Sheila was dead. Mom would make her wake up. No, it was too late. She was cold. She was gone. Mom would wake her up. The two sides slapped back and forth in my head.

She had Mimi with her. She must have pulled her out of junior high.

"The ambulance is on the way and so is C de Baca," she told Bucky as she rushed through the kitchen to Sheila's bedroom. I rose up and followed. Maybe I was mistaken, maybe Sheila was breathing.

We rushed back inside Sheila's bedroom, a quiet, still place, tidy, the land of 'a place for everything and everything in its place', the mantra of compulsive behavior. The first thing I saw was Dad kneeling on the floor, holding Sheila's hand and sobbing. I forgot to get the really sharp kitchen knife in the kitchen. I wanted to stab him and now I couldn't. Bucky and Mimi were in front of me and they would have never let me get past them if I went to kill him. How quick that thought of the knife came in and out of my mind because I could hear Sheila's voice inside my head. "Make him give it all to you and Bucky and Mimi. Take it away from him, make him pay. Make him give you the ranch." It was crazy.

Mom put her hands on Sheila's face and whimpered this strange high pitched moan. She fell atop the bed and took Sheila into her arms, rocking and repeating, "Wake up, my baby girl, come on, wake up." We all starting crying then, me and Bucky, Dad, mom. I hugged onto Mimi, frozen in the doorway. I put hand around her shoulders. She yanked away. She was stone. She was in don't-touch-me mode. I knew where that came from. Suddenly with guilt I realized that I knew when it happened. At the beginning of summer, five months ago, that's when Mimi had become stone and wouldn't let anyone touch her, not a hug, not allowing a sisterly gentle brush-away of an out of place lock of hair, not a pat on the hand or a squeeze of pride. She would recoil as if we all had thorns growing out of our skin. Both Mimi's hands covered her mouth.

We heard the ambulance siren coming all fourteen miles down the county road from the interstate. It announced our shame to everyone who lived on the road. It was open country and all the ranchers could hear the sound. A siren was rare, especially one coming all the way down the county road. Everyone would be listening for where it stopped. Sheila's siren of inevitability blew all the way from town and ended in a rattle of gravel as the ambulance pulled up in front of the ranch house. The sheriff's car came right behind. Doors slammed and Dad moved past us to open the front door and direct the men inside.

No chance now to go get a rifle and load it. I couldn't get the Colt revolver out of the case in the living room. The sheriff was here, damn him. Sheriff Ernesto Cabeza de Baca wouldn't let me put bullets into the evil monster who stole our cheesy childhoods and gobbled them greedily, the rat monster who put his hands all over us. The man who spit on his own children. He wouldn't die anyway just to be mean, I remember Sheila saying to me, really think about it, Carla, make him give you all the ranch in exchange for not testifying at the coroner's hearing. Make him sign papers. Do it.

What an interesting idea. If I testified and I showed the note, there would be charges. Not murder charges, but enough these days to get him 15 years in prison. I don't know how I got so smart so quick. I mean, I barely made it out of high school three years ago. I got that job with H& R Block as a receptionist and then the H& R Block boss and his nice wife who were both CPAs taught me bookkeeping. It was pretty straightforward work, clean, clear, and fairly easy once you understood the basics. I took three community college courses. I was good at it. All I had to do was show up in an office on time, dress in the cleanest town clothes and proceed straight-forward to live in a world of numbers. Eventually I found a roommate situation so I could move off Mom's couch. I also read the newspaper every morning at 6 a.m. with two cups of coffee. Every section, I heard Sheila say proudly. I liked best following murder stories from arrest to the verdict. I once thought it would be interesting to be a court clerk or a justice of the peace. I couldn't do anything farfetched right away, how would I start to get there I mean, because --- and here I heard Sheila speak again, what she always harping on, the family explanation for why everything went wrong --- because there is poison in us.

Before Sheila died, I did not know how to get the poison out, how to erase, eradicate, expunge, excavate, decrete, delete. Neither did Sheila, and we talked about it a lot. I know it hurt her something awful and her seeing that shrink made it worse. On those days she raged and cried so hard. Yet nothing changed. She would feed the horses and he'd show up and she'd have to blast around him.

The only antidote that made sense now was punishment. Yes. I was going to take away his land. I felt stronger with this purpose. There comes a time when purpose is stronger than terror.

Bucky spoke up loud and told C de Baca there was no suicide note. The family secret works like a clean machine. Together we stared down Dad who didn't contradict.

In the week that followed, I needed help from a lawyer who I met when I worked on his books. I unfolded my plan after Mimi and Mom's therapy session. There was me, Bucky, Mom, Mimi. Plus the lawyer and two assistants that I had sit out in the car until it was time for me to call them in. I went back inside, down the hall to Sheila's bedroom and everybody watching. I opened the door to her bedroom. It stayed open while we sat around the dining table and presented Dad with the ultimatum, full disclosure, criminal charges, a certainty of civil suits, and papers to sign. A lot of publicity. He could even go to jail, there was that possibility.

He roared, I will not lie to you. He roared, he raged, he broke a chair. He even cried. I did what their therapist had taught us, each of us --- how to say no without explanation because that keeps the power. We stayed firm on the ultimatum. He had to own up to what he did and not own the land.

At one point Bucky went into the kitchen and got the pot of coffee. Mom served cups to everyone. She didn't sit beside Dad and she didn't say much. One by one we would go separately into the kitchen to cry. That's how it went mostly. We had to pass by Sheila's bedroom to go back to the living room. I touched the bedroom door with my cheek before returning. I miss her so.

We stayed firm in our ultimatum. We did what had to be done. Mimi kept her hand over her mouth until the moment that we heard her clear voice, "Sign it or I go to C de Baca." That's how it went down. All of a sudden he agreed. I was actually shocked. He said, "I don't want it anymore, I don't want anything to do with any one of ya's."

Then I went outside and told the lawyers it was time for them to stop earning money by sitting in the car and to come inside to earn it. No, not really. I was nice. They went in, he signed and it was notarized and taken away to be copied and filed and all done, private agreement and a bill of sale. We drove in separate cars all the way to the bank. We went in, he signed some more papers.

Afterward we got Sheila's ashes and drove all the way back to the ranch. There was my car, Bucky's Dodge Ram, mom's Taurus, dad's Jeep, all in a line going down the county road. No sirens for Sheila this time, only quiet hot tears. I almost drove off the road once for sobbing. We brought Sheila's ashes to the top of the butte. He only made it two-thirds of the way up, sat on a boulder, all slumped and emptied. I almost felt sad for him. The truth is, I was only sad for Sheila. She missed out on the rest of her life.

Some good rancher neighbors had already climbed up there and were waiting for us and Sheila's three good friends were up there too. The whole community at the top of what we started to call from that point forward Sheila's Butte. We were close to the sky and looking out over a small piece of land, a huge horizon that included a couple of mountain ranges, a couple of mesas, a lot of arroyos like cracks in the earth, the dots of piñon bushes, the dark county road, the small ranch house, the tiny windows of the ranch house, the cattle and horses small as toys, the entire stretch of earth moving toward the horizon and that horizon like a giant pair of scissors cutting off the past and the present. We looked out over the entire ranch. We looked out at tomorrow. We took handfuls of Sheila and threw them into the air and her grey dust had the pretty lightness and swirlyness of smoke. Gone very quickly. We did a lot of crying and lot of hugging. The pain was tremendous, like lightning cracking through the heart and pulverizing its little pieces of glass. I was angry then.

If it wasn't for hearing Sheila's voice on the day that made me forever lonely, I would still be violent and angry. All right, maybe I am still angry. I will learn forgiveness as my life goes forward, on its own trail, in its own time.

Sheila just plain hurt too much. That's what I told everybody after Dad descended from the butte. He was in a big hurry to get off that pile of rocks. He slipped on scree and hopped from one boulder to another and got down without looking back.

He moved to Alberta, Canada. Or somewhere like that. Who cares. This is the last I'll be talking about him. Good to get it out. A real disinfectant cleaning. Only it doesn't really work like that, but we want it to. Forgiving and forgetting, two completely different matters.

Bucky wanted the ranch house. He got it very easy, because I sure didn't want that museum of dark memories. I scraped a road on the back acreage, had a well drilled, and built a nice adobe. Now when I look out my kitchen window I can see Sheila's Butte and imagine Roy Orbison singing and all of us dancing, twirling skirts and happy after a holiday dinner. Mom and Mimi set it up for Bucky to range his cattle on their acreage in exchange for meat. Just last week I climbed up the butte and hung an aluminum Christmas star on a piñon bush near where we scattered her ashes.

I had a good cry there, I miss her so much. It has quite a view up there, all the sky, all the land and all the horizons are far enough away that she can be out there waiting for us to finish up living. Sheila is a particularly good part of me. She makes me strong enough to figure things out as I go on, on my own.

~~ The End ~~

WILD RELEASE

I

There are no clean getaways where family is involved. The three small brass bells affixed to the kitchen door in the Milliano household took care of that. The three bells, each two inches in diameter, were set into a flat iron bar about eight inches long and the whole fastened to the top of the kitchen door leading to a brick patio. Antique, collectible, unique, the bells were once part of sled gear from 1880s New York City wintertime in Central Park where horse and an open carriage on slender skids slid gaily across the snowy meadowlands. Now the ringing brass trio was a fixture in the household of the Millianos, antiques collectors and parents of two teenage daughters, all recently relocated to the outskirts of Santa Fe. Mother and Father Milliano chose the Hispanic latitudes and high desert altitudes of northern New Mexico to better, in their words, "get away from certain people" and build the perfect house complete with an attached antique shop. The latter was a New England-style dream and the former --- getting away from people --- was peculiar to the personalities involved. There were certain New York relatives whose violent arguments with Father Milliano had escalated to a level hardly stoppable even by the police. Besides, it was 1965 and the world seemed to be going mad with war, protests, strange ideas and a rising cost of living. The impetus was to try new things. Maybe the outskirts of Santa Fe was a good choice; maybe not.

Hearing the jingling sleigh bells on the kitchen door did not budge the home owners from the front porch where in the early evening they were watching a gorgeous southwest sunset. In their maple rocking chairs, Mr. and Mrs. Milliano, the collectors of Early Americana who were kicking off a new life as antiques dealers, reposed on a flagstone loggia which substituted for a proper New England porch. The bells signaled that the dinner dishes had been washed by the eldest daughter, Veronica, that she had dried the dishes, swept the floor and was now bringing the dog's food outside to the patio where the pooch was chained to a small, roughly constructed dog coop covered in black tarpaper. Nightly Veronica tended to these tasks in their required order. Nightly she cleaned the kitchen after dinner and fed Jingo the dog his mushy Gravy Train.

In the glow of a red and orange western sky, she watched Jingo eat heartily from the soup-pot sized portion. To stuff him well before the night arrived with its high altitude chill, she had added a third of a loaf of cheap white bread, torn up and mixed with the dog food nuggets and hot water. This was his only meal of the day. The savory doggie stew steamed in the onset of cool twilight; and although the dog food aroma was faintly unpleasant to her, Veronica watched the rising tendrils of steam evaporate in the dry atmosphere amidst the slobber of the dog's eating. She noticed how quickly the steam tendrils lifted above Jingo's head and escaped, rising skyward of their own nature and disappearing How contrary to her own life, she grimly reflected, a life unnaturally compressed like a sour-smelling latex balloon in a closet. Here she was, hopeless and lost, an uncomfortable 18, working full-time as a telephone operator, and turning her paychecks over to her parents every two weeks. No yearnings, no reach; and in this new outpost, no social life, no friends. Only the devoted companionship of a fierce-looking dog which Father commanded must be chained outside.

Jingo had been with their family for a year. He was a medium sized mixed breed from the Animal Shelter, a strong dog with dark fur and a broad, tight chest. He had upright ears and long legs. He was easily excitable, loyal, adventurous and, despite his hunger, quite wild with the expectation that Veronica the family rebel would soon unclip his chain. He had accompanied Veronica on long walks across the open ranch country and, being a creature of uncomplicated habit, he expected more of the same.

Veronica gave some thought now in the cooling twilight, how she and Jingo made beelines to nowhere and back on her days off work and sometimes late at night, across the dry prairie and into the foothills --- meandering between the stunted clumps of buffalo grass, around dark piñon bushes, making footprints in the soft sand down the center of dry gulches called arroyos, and running uphill again, dodging little knee-high cactus. Together they had done this many times in various directions and never once encountered another human being nor another dog on these day and night forays into the vast landscape of the west. And they both seemed to have an invisible elastic string attached to their backs in order to return precisely where they began. Invisible bindings, undeclared longings and silent miseries stapled their routines to the center of a circle.

Father said Jingo was part dingo dog of Australia. Both Veronica and Betty looked at pictures in a library book of dingo dogs and saw little to no resemblance. Dingo dogs are sand colored, skinny and feral. Veronica and Betty kept this information undeclared for it was best never to disagree with Father. Grave consequences would ensue, sometimes involving beatings. Once, in reaction to tv news about the Viet

Nam war protests, Father broke every lamp in the living room, upturned the dining table and dumped the kitchen garbage onto Veronica's freshly mopped floor. He possessed a volatile and unpredictable energy, like an engine ignited by emotional explosions. Best not to watch the tv news with him. Better safe than sorry. Better low profile than vocal.

Veronica unclipped Jingo's heavy chain which fell onto the brick patio with loud clinks. The dog bolted and raced many times around the outside perimeter of the entire house at full speed, a dark blur of strength, a devil wind in the twilight. Loud voices issued from the front porch.

"God damn it all to hell. She let that dog loose again."

"Let him go," Mother replied. "He has to run sometime. Don't get up."

"I told her never to unchain him. I'll beat the crap out of her for doing this and she knows it." Father rose with a sneer at his wife's request and went back inside the house. He yanked open the kitchen door with a loud jangling crash and yelled. "I told you never to let that dog loose."

Veronica herself bolted around to the far side of the house calling happily, "Jingie, Jingie, Jingie. Come on now." There was not much volume in her yells.

Father shouted a command to tie up the dog right away. He returned to the porch, the bells once again resounding in a combined shrill as he shut the door furiously behind him.

The house was shaped like an H with a bedroom wing and an antiques shop wing. These were connected by the middle bar of the letter, a section which contained a large combination kitchen-dining room, a living room, and the front porch. It had been built to resemble an eastern suburban house with peaked roof, wooden siding, and knotty pine interior. Indeed, the entire house had been built over the course of ten months by the family of four, Mr. and Mrs. Milliano and their teenage daughters Veronica and Betty; and it had been a formidable task, dusty and bitter work involving a lot of bruises, sweat and tears. There were some good times, a few laughs and certainly swells of pride in the visual evidence of accomplishment as studded walls rose, windows set in place, and the roof shingled. There were also unforgettable times of great bickering and fatigue. And there were times of sheer exhaustion, frustration, and figurative whip-cracking. Breaks were rare.

How often they heard, "I'll teach you what work means, you lazy sons a bitches. That's what you need. Not boyfriends or new dresses or reading magazines in the bathroom. You need to learn what real work is."

Now the house was finished. Its appearance was an anomaly in the land of adobe enchantment where the norm was square-ish mud colored homes with window frames painted ultramarine blue or deep orange or intense yellow. Father hated adobe for he didn't know how to use it. He hated things he knew and things he didn't know and he spent a lot of time on the porch after dinner contemplating his resentments. Mother stuck by him.

Betty was 13. She stayed in her bedroom a lot with the door locked. She dashed off to the school bus at an early hour, made a appearance at the dinner table, and kept a low profile during weekends. She continued and intensified this pattern until shortly after her high school graduation when she met and married a policeman who handled a minor auto accident involving her vehicle. "Are you all right?" he had asked as he leaned in the driver's window. "Yes," she replied sweetly, "now that you're here." And the two of them galloped away into the sunset, over the horizon, into new lives, rarely to return.

That was the future. Now Jingo raced to Betty's bedroom window and batted the glass with his nose. Betty opened the window and let him jump inside. She fed him cookies and, giggling, tossed one outside to get him to leap back through the open window again. She shut the window and drew the curtain just as Veronica reached that side of the house.

II

Veronica was given a job as a long distance telephone operator in the telephone exchange located one block from the plaza in downtown Santa Fe. She was a bit brain-numb and frightened when she applied. They let her take the application home to complete it. Two weeks after starting work, Mother told her it was time to buy a car and selected a red Volkswagen bug for Veronica. She showed Veronica where to sign for the new car loan of $1,800. The telephone company paid her $1.25 an hour, minimum wage. Mother allotted her gas money, the car payment, and a small savings for college someday.

The telephone company gave Veronica a split shift and odd weekdays off. She worked from 10 a.m. to 2 p.m. and returned to work from 6 p.m. to 10 p.m. To wile away the four hour break, she drove slowly along circuitous and unpaved roads throughout northern New Mexico. She kept all the car windows rolled down. Sometimes on these county roads she stopped, cut the engine and sat listening. Occasional winds buffeted the car, a bird trilled its elegant song somewhere far from the road, and the wordless call of improbable freedom beckoned with the hypnotism of the great open spaces. Her eyes habitually sought the significant horizon line, drawn as strong as a pencil line in between the sky and the land; it compelled her toward a vast and welcoming space and wrote impossible, erasable notes to Veronica. The invitations read, Come and Live Your Life. Come Further Away. A Little More Now, Come On.

Sometimes the dun-colored caleche soil was dark and wet. A rain storm would have passed over within the last hour and an acrid dusty smell pervade the air. Creosote. In this solitude she could feel her ears ring and her heart beat and her nose sense something new. Eternally concentric circles surrounded her, ripples in a pond of sage round her car, piñon, cane cholla, Russian olive trees, sage, chamisa. She watched the sky plow enormous thicknesses of clouds, shoving them swiftly across the land toward purple mountains majesty, just like the song. Veronica liked the west. It was an open doorway.

One day after his pot of Gravy Train was eaten and his chain released, Jingo raced wildly around the house and jumped through the open window of the red Volkswagen bug. He sat down in the passenger seat facing forward, pink tongue hanging from the side of his mouth, panting heavily and focusing intently on the view through the windshield. He sat quite solidly in the passenger seat, adamant and communicating with a thumping tail.

"So you want to go for a ride with me, Jingo?" Veronica yielded easily, started the car and drove around the house in a big circle.

"You're ruining the lawn, god damn it all to hell." Father shouted from the front porch.

"There is no lawn," her mother complained from the side of her mouth. "There's never going to be a lawn. They haven't heard of lawns here. Let her go. You want another beer?"

Veronica and Jingo drove round and round the H house atop the dusty caleche and across the cow-pie clumps of buffalo grass.

"Stop it now," Father hollered on her second circuit. "We don't want tracks any more. We're through building."

"We'll never be through," Mother complained again, flatly. "We've still got to drywall inside the antiques shop. When are we ever going to get that done?"

"We're through. Enough is enough. Shut up about it."

"There's centipedes and termites munching on the foundations as we sit here. Look up. Don't bother with her. Look up there. They've already made their marks on the wood along the eaves. I tell you, I hate to go up to the attic anymore. This is not a climate for attics. They drop down from the roof. All these desert insects eat wood and we went and built them a buffet."

"Get her to stop. She's going nuts."

At Veronica's second circuit, Betty came to her open window to watch. She held a Spanish Language textbook against her chest and shook her head slowly. On the third pass, she tossed a cookie to Jingo as Veronica inched the car very close to the window. Betty raised her voice over the noise of the car engine, "You're pitiful. They say you're acting nuts. You better stop before he blows up. Besides you're stirring up the dust too much." She shut her window and receded into the dim interior.

On the porch resignation mixed with distraction. "Doesn't she have to go back to work soon?"

"She'll stop. It's five thirty already and she has to be there by six fifteen. You going to the union hall tomorrow morning?"

The antiques were not selling. Slowly Mother and Father discovered that few in New Mexico followed the New England pattern of driving into the countryside on weekends to sniff out antiques in barns along the roadsides. Here there were no bucolic red barns along the roadsides, only distant mesas, ancient ruins, barbed wire, grazing cattle and horses. There was a different history to New Mexico, a history unrelated to Pilgrims, the first colonies and the Revolutionary War. In recourse, Mr. Milliano had to seek work in his standby trade, carpentry.

"Sons of bitches. Everything in that union hall is si-si-si. They talk their Spanish and I never know what they're saying. The best jobs go to primos, their cousins. If I don't go every morning to the union hall I'll be put at the bottom of the list again. They gotta send me on that bridge job by Raton that's coming up."

"You said that starts in the spring. That's months away."

"I go when I go. Shut up about it. I'm the only one who knows hot steel and that pays better than framing so you ought to be happy. They have to send me, primo or no primo. They don't know jack shit about hot steel. They only know adobe. Houses made out of dirt."

"Why did we come here from the east? It's like living on the moon."

"Don't start. We're not going back."

"I just don't know how I can cook dinner and feed this family with no money coming in. It's all going out."

"I said shut up about it."

The red bug drove past one last time.

Father shook his fist, "Veronica! You hear what I said?"

"Tell her it's time to go to work."

"You're marking up the front of the property with tire tracks!" He turned away from the dust cloud. "These kids don't care, god damn it."

"We'll use her paycheck until spring. Then she should go to college and make something of herself. She's the smart one. The other, who knows? She only makes C's. She never studies."

III

On her next day off Veronica took Jingo all the way into Santa Fe. They drove up to the top of Canyon Road to admire the quaking aspens and returned slowly along the Santa Fe River to the plaza downtown. Jingo waited in the car while she filled the bug's tank of gas at 25 cents a gallon, returned library books, and purchased a small bag of roasted piñon nuts from an old man standing in front of the bank. She wandered a little around the plaza. Indians sat on blanket-draped milk cartons under the shady portico of a history museum and sold turquoise jewelry, pottery and silverwork they had made and spread out on striped wool blankets, tablecloths and pieces of velvet. The vendors were intelligent people, fun people, who, she discovered, lived in their own community on land belonging to them from forever and not more than twenty miles from the H house. She bought three dry corn necklaces made of brightly dyed corn kernels strung on sewing thread and fashioned with a buckskin tie. She chose dark pink, orange and turquoise green. The vendor and his teenage daughter invited her to visit their community to watch the winter Corn Dance on New Years Day. She shook her head, "I'll probably have to work."

She did not tell the family about conversations with new friends. The few times she had done so was disastrous. Father stiffened and squinted at her suspiciously as if she had done something wrong. He would ask questions that she could never answer good enough not to lead into more questions about what those people wanted from her, why were they really interested in her.

He would work up to a rant that if she had time to meet new people it meant she wasn't working hard enough because there was too much to do right now at the house to waste time dawdling in town just to shoot the breeze. And Mother would lecture that she "stay with your own kind. Who knows how those people live? You shouldn't be meeting anyone we don't know. You're too young to understand what they want from you."

Thus the pageantry of her good experiences remained secretive, kept behind a shut door just like Betty's. An anguished murk remained deep inside, disturbingly omnipresent. She could not find an end, a pressure release for her turbulent emotions, the fears, anxiety, longing, frustration, with occasional unspoken fury masking all those feelings. Distractions and extremes ruled. She would race and dawdle, cut the engine on lonely roads --- and the next day drive home from work after 10 p.m. at twenty, thirty miles over the speed limit. She began to smoke cigarettes rapidly, lighting one from the stub of the last. At dinner she seldom refused Mother's offer of Kahlua poured generously over ice cream for dessert.

There was one fine relief. When she went for a drive into Santa Fe with Jingo, Veronica made a point to stop on the way back at the Fosters Freeze on the outskirts of Cerrillos Road. There she would buy two large vanilla frozen custard cones. One she held out for Jingo in the passenger seat to lick, gulp and consume heartily to the surprising cheers of people young and old waiting in line. Afterward Jingo stared until Veronica could not eat any more of her own cone and she would yield the remainder to him. One day as she held the cone for him, she took a good look at the rough exterior of his unwashed dark fur, gray-bristled jowls, yellowed and broken teeth, large deep brown eyes, steely strong legs and paws. She saw her knight, a noble creature in trying circumstances, wearing battle armor and consigned occasionally to dungeons and strange lands. She smiled and set her shoulders differently. The atmosphere in the Fosters Freeze parking lot was always light, sunshiny bright, facing west with warmth pouring through the windshield. There were usually customers waiting in line before the order window, wearing ordinary, colorful clothing, cowboys, students, Navajos, Chicanos, mothers in ruffly blouses, dusty workmen, children with thick dark hair and after-school gaiety playing and chattering in Spanish, all happy in expectation of an ice cream treat. Gaiety prevailed. And Jingo was the king and center of attention as he ate his ice cream, a goofy dog invisibly dressed in dark conquistador leather, fierce as the ages, ravenous as history. As she hugged him afterward, her cheek felt the warmth and softness of his ears.

When she went to work for her shift at the telephone exchange, she parked near the Cathedral along Alameda beside the narrow stony creek of the Santa Fe River and went inside a windowless two-story building through an unmarked steel door. Up a beige stairwell and a left turn into an operators lounge filled with lockers, a plastic couch, ashtrays, a few mismatched chairs and a wall clock. Veronica placed her purse inside a small beige locker sadly reminiscent of her old high school locker, snapped her combination lock into place and twirled its black face once. On the minute she joined four or five other operators heading single file down the hallway into the board room, and took her headset from a pegboard in the hallway as she passed. The headset's heavy long electric cord, wrapped in brown rayon, had a peculiar two-prong plug which she was not allowed to swing. Notices were posted along the hallway forbidding this careless treatment of telephone company property. No Swinging Cords. She drew a mental pencil X through the 'w'.

Each shift took place in the Operators Room, enormous, rectangular, thirty feet long. Along each side of the room a "phone board" or five foot tall dark panel rose above long, narrow tables. These long tables were divided into twenty operator stations each station fitted with a connector for the headset plug and matched with an armless secretarial chair on wheels. The tall phone board was divided into long horizontal lines of holes, some lit to indicate either phone circuits in use or ringing requests for operator assistance.

Tiny lettering identified groups of holes --- Taos, Pecos, Espanola, Tierra Amarilla, Glorieta, Pecos, Los Alamos, Raton --- all the lovely and musical sounding names of northern New Mexico.

Between the chair and the board were a dozen metal tips resembling rifle bullets that stood upright on the table. These tips were attached to more brown rayon-covered cords which unrolled from beneath the table as she pulled up on the metal bullet and plugged it into a lit hole on the board in front of her.

"Operator," she spoke rapidly into her mouthpiece.

The word came out like Op-er-der. Veronica faithfully mimicked this pronunciation from all the other women --- men were not hired as operators ---- seated along the length of an endless table wearing headsets and dressed in suits, silk blouses, business dresses, high heels, and regulation pantyhose. It was forbidden to come barelegged to work. Professional attire required. Operators would be sent home to change, suffering unpaid hours, if they did not wear stockings or pantyhose. Socks and fishnet stockings were also inappropriate work attire. Operators were not allowed to swing their chairs from side to side as in wiggling, nor rest elbows on the table as in slumping. There were other rules equally mundane and annoying to Veronica. Speaking to another operator was forbidden since the customer might overhear. Keeping the wheels of one's chair in exact alignment with the wheels of the chairs of the other operators was a rule strictly enforced by a few overbearing supervisors who wardened hawkish both the rule of silence and the rule of correctly positioned chair legs.

To take one hundred calls an hour was the highest goal. The numbers were posted weekly near the headset pegboard along the hallway that ran in two directions, to work and to freedom. Month after month Veronica's numbers rose as she quickly learned to take as many calls as she could possibly handle in order to make her time pass in a snap. An ulterior motivation began to develop. Veronica took calls swiftly in order to listen to a great variety of voices, which, she discovered, pleased her as much as listening to the wind and birds. The voices of the people from somewhere out there in the enchanted atmosphere, beneath the turquoise sky, between the purple mountains majesty, among the random clumps of piñon bushes, across the canyons and broad prairie and at home in adobes built of soft mud with window frames painted blue.

"Operator, I would like to place a person to person call to Mr. Henry Gonzales in Los Angeles at area code 213. The number is ..."

"Your number please." Veronica responded while scribbling the information on a 3x5 order pad, as taught, precisely as taught, in the training room during her first week at work. "Your name please."

No other words could be used. The trainer stressed that there was to be absolutely no variations on these phrases. And only designated operators were allowed to reply in Spanish. If the caller spoke in Spanish to the operator, Veronica was to raise her arm immediately to alert a supervisor in order to pass the call speedily, within seconds, so the caller would not even realize that a change had occurred. The customers were handled as gently as babies.

The customers, the voices, sat at the ends of long telephone lines, across miles of great lengths of sagging lines held up by sturdy poles --- and attentively listened to the voices of the op-er-ders --- and both ends wondered and imagined and squinted at the unseen. Was it all so ordinary? Or was it magical?

Each and every telephone call was regarded as a serious matter, regulated by federal law, and subject to absolute confidentiality and considered a strong part of national security --- or some other combination of those high-sounding phrases --- Veronica was reminded in posters on the walls in the long hallway. During her second week Veronica was required to read a single sheet of paper stating those high sounding phrases, and to sign a different sheet of paper stating that she was a loyal U.S. citizen who had read the first paper. Obeying without a peep or a blink, she signed her name in a rolling, youthful hand and silently considered that having done so, the paper would now be carried to a locked file drawer as evidence of vitally useless importance for someone of authority, someone perhaps wearing dark, stiff clothing and carrying a name badge and working in a windowless room behind a plain metal door. In the back of her mind Veronica imagined the voice of the comedian Professor Irwin Corey explaining with a pointer how, now, at this moment and juncture of time, this someone of authority in his dark suit, behind the plain metal door now has the two pieces of paper and knows that she knows of confidentiality and vital telecommunications security, yes he knows, and knows that she knows, knows that he knows that she knows, ad infinitum, quid pro quo, quidquid latine dictum sit altum viditur, and so on and so forth; although of what it meant she was uncertain but he, the man behind the plain metal door had learned a little bit about everything and an awful lot about very little and it adds up bit by bit so that at the end of his life he would know an tremendous lot about absolutely nothing. Just a jumble of large words filling up the room and cluttering the locked file drawer. Telecommunications Confidentiality - Vital To National Security - Breach Of Secrecy - Punished To The Severest Extent.

Two minutes later she began her training as an information operator. She sat facing two phonebooks positioned upright in front of her and looked up numbers for customers by using a ruler and rubber caps on her thumb and index finger. No magic to that, but there were rules. For example, there was one correct way to turn the page of a phone book, at the one o'clock position on the right-side page, drawing the hand down slowly so as not to rip a page. The instructor made sure that Veronica learned to do it just so.

Again, the job was boring; the voices interesting. Everyone had to dial "O" for long distance calls in 1965 and even did so for emergencies, house fires and accidents. There was a hole on the back board labeled City Police and another for Fire and several for the hospital. There was no direct long distance dialing. Alas, the person–to-person call was a grand refinement of service to be discarded in the future. On a person–to-person call if the person requested could not come to the phone, there was no charge and a callback name and number could be left for a return collect call that was luxuriously never indicated as collect; instead, the operator smartly announced like a butler, "Your person-to-person call to Mr. King is ready now." The customers got hip and a person-to-person call became a device for letting the distant family members know that someone arrived back home safely after a visit, especially since in the west it took hours to drive from one town to the next. Make the call, on the other end state no, not here now, hang up, message of safe arrival transmitted for free.

Veronica discerned a ringing silence in the spaces between words. She was able to hear a live line, to perceive electricity, and to hear the wind swinging the lines looped between the sturdy poles running along the roadsides, the great vast spaces of the southwest.

Two hours answering calls, then a small break to smoke two Virginia Slims cigarettes in the operators lounge, read a chapter of a novel, then two more hours. She took covertly thrilling calls from Abiquiu, Wagon Mound, Questa, Dixon, Clayton, Velarde, Peñasco, mysterious names and places of pre-Colombian antiquity, Hispanic, Navajo and covered wagon history, places of rug-weavers and gunfighter adventure. The customers' names had beautiful, soft syllables, Garcia, Duran, Lujan, Moran, Cabeza de Baca, Carson.

To while away the hours at the exchange she imagined the appearance of the owners of the voices at the end of the line. She thought of black rubbery cord slung from pole to pole across the vast plains, up and down the bluish purple snow capped mountains and strung from corners of adobe homes, clusters of flat-topped homes in old pueblos that stretched back, continuously inhabited from the year 8000 BC. Older than America which dated from the American Revolution more or less, or broadly the 1700s. The lights lit and her hands moved habitually to plug the holes, announce op-er-der, note and rotary-dial the requested numbers, announcing the person-to-persons, toggling a little upright switch on the table to speak or privately listen to the first five seconds of the call in assurance that the connection was true. Veronica dreamed. She loved those five seconds of non-confidentiality. She gleaned the other ways to live in a family.

It's yours, Jimmy …
I'm so glad to hear …
It's me, Dad …
Hello my love, how are you?
Oh my dear I'm sorry to have to tell you …
Hey honey …
Querido, como estás?…
Mikey, it's Mom …
Hey did you get what I sent you …
How you doin' …
Hi, is everything okay over there?

All the voices calling from a place where land meets sky, a place where the Navajo scissors cut the open horizon, the proffering origin of all voices of male, female, young, old, loving, formal, haughty, groveling, light, husky, portentous of good news and bad. These initial snippets of conversation left their imprint with Veronica. She contrived a quick picture in her mind for each speaker, usually pleasant, sometimes somber, possibly tall or short, young or old, light complexion or dark, bright-hearted or weary.

Beneath her own olive skin the beginnings of restlessness amplified. She was eighteen years old and had a glimpse, albeit sightless, of worlds beyond her own, a five-second signal light blinking in the bruised darkness. Coming from the horizon, the callers' signal passed through and circled her in a small mobius of light before moving into infinity. These transmittals juiced her and got Veronica ready like an airplane with its motor running, wheel chocks in place, surging forward and upward.

"Where's the paycheck? I want to go into town and get it cashed."

For the first time Veronica felt a surge of ownership. She turned slowly.

"I mean now. Hurry up."

Numbly Veronica opened her whip-stitched purse made of honey-colored hard leather stamped with Western designs of tiny horseshoes and diamonds with starry rays. She found her pink plastic wallet and slipped the paycheck from the billfold section. Without looking at Mother she handed over the long pale paper to her mother. She knew what protest would bring. Trouble. Punishment. Days before the argument faded. Last month's Betty's clavicle was broken by a blow from Father during an argument about dating.

Month after month Veronica moved with the tick of a clock through phone company shifts at the exchange. She bought gas and ice creams for Jingo and only gazed into the windows of stores around the plaza. She visited the jewelry vendors, her Santo Domingo acquaintances. She did go inside Woolworth's Five and Ten store once to buy a Frito Pie for thirty cents, which was a tasty local snack; a small bag of Frito corn chips, the bag cut open and a ladleful of spicy red chile plopped in. She visited the large stone cathedral. She gazed into the fabulous windows of Packard's Trading Post, a turquoise store full of gorgeous, award-winning necklaces and bracelets, the blue, white and red prize ribbons alongside price tags in the thousands of dollars. Beyond the window display she could see that inside Packard's there were shelves chock full of colorful Navajo blankets, black pottery from San Ildefonso and brown and white pottery from other pueblos. She imagined the hands that made these beautiful things, hands belonging to people with voices who used telephones sometimes.

When Veronica checked out books from the downtown library around the corner from the Palace of the Governors she spoke no more than pat phrases. Yes, it's a lovely day. Thank you. Park the car, walk up the telephone company steps, plug bullet-tipped cords into lit holes, take a break in the operator's lounge, smoke a cigarette or two, and home again to clean the kitchen, feed Jingo, read herself to sleep. She immersed herself in complicated novels by Leo Tolstoy, Feodor Dostoyevsky and Sigrid Undset. These stories came to resolution. History drew her out of herself, also. She read Frank Waters' Masked Gods, The Land of Poco Tiempo by Charles Lummis, and Winter In Taos by Mabel Dodge Lujan. She read Sea of Grass and Black Elk Speaks. There were other ways to do things, other ways to live, other worlds.

She stopped coming home during the four hours before the resumption of her split shift. Instead she explored the town that was founded, or named, in 1607 by merchants and settlers and soldiers from Mexico, Spain and Missouri. In the bug she drove slowly many times back and forth along Bishop's Lodge Road and Acequia Madre Street, gazing at the intermittent homes and open fields. She wandered the uphill reaches of Canyon Road, a touristy compilation of art shops and sculpture galleries and glass blowers; and drove very slowly the long east-west length of Rodeo Road, an unpaved street on the outskirts of Santa Fe, past its large arena and grandstand, past a veterinary clinic with horse corrals in the rear, and continued through where Rodeo Road became empty on both sides with dips and little hills to connect the northeasterly Las Vegas highway with the southerly interstate to Albuquerque in a local's shortcut. It was one of her favorite drives during the break between shifts. The views were serene. The dirt road was bumpy enough to go slow and fly her gaze higher, toward the yellowing aspens in the autumn mountains of the Sangre de Cristo range.

She bought a road map of New Mexico at a gas station beside the interstate and began exploring nearby towns of La Conchita, Cochiti, Glorieta, Pecos. She drove through Pojoaque repeating the name and enjoying its pronunciation with the lips like a kiss. There Willa Cather's Archbishop retired after constructing his cathedral in Santa Fe. She visited the sleepy town of Española and wondered about its family secrets, Hispanic and Indian.

She slipped away on her next day off to explore Chimayo's place of miracles, El Santuario. She left early, before the others in the H house arose, cupping her hand over the bells as she opened the kitchen door. The route took her north of Santa Fe through Tesuque along windy blind curves between hills. She recalled the photos in the newspapers of people along the sides of the highway walking in procession or moving on their knees in an annual pilgrimage to this place of miracles. She was amazed at the distance they had committed to travel, astounding perseverance, life changing experience.

All previous church gardeners were buried in the front courtyard of El Santuario's tiny church, a tender tribute that touched her and indicated the depth of compassion within Mexican culture. A long, side room of the church was filled with crutches and notes tacked and taped on the walls, messages of prayers, requests, gratitudes in stricken handwriting. In the tiny, holy alcove, Veronica touched the small mound of soft, sacred sand on the floor and knelt to say a prayer. She prayed, Let Me Know Where I'm Going --- Help Me --- I'm Caught In A Circle --- Protect Me --- Protect My Family --- Help Me Do My Job At Work And Not Make A Mistake --- Get Everyone To Stop Being Angry At Me All The Time --- Don't Let My Car Break Down --- Help Me Not Be Lonely --- Please Dear God --- Make Everything Stop Exploding Over And Over Again.

She had been calm until this prayer. She trembled uncontrollably at the realization of her unhappiness and could not breathe. Within scant moments she thought she would faint, absorbed into a bright loss of self and cease-to-exist-ness. The sensation receded into a haunt of troubling thoughts in the back of her mind. Someone touched her on the shoulder. Startled, she inhaled. It was a pilgrim politely asking to take a turn kneeling before the sacred sand. Veronica yielded humbly.

As she returned to her daily pattern of work, home, horizon-staring, Veronica carried a secret, that the prospect of change had become inevitable. She was moving into the realm, the day, when enough is enough. Now, familiar rooms seemed narrower. Father's voice and his footsteps made a panicky knot rise in her throat. Stillness but for her job. Away from the operators room she scarcely spoke and made no friends. She already knew too well that if she strayed, she would be chased.

That's what happened a year earlier when she ran away in the dark time of crying jags and sleepless misery, before she began work at the telephone company, while they had been under his whip, building the house. Often, back then, she seemed to sob for days while digging endless, deep ditches for water, sewer and gas pipes. She ran away one Saturday afternoon during that dark time, late, about 6 p.m. After dinner she had gone outside, put down the pot of food for Jingo and kept going, left the property and kept to the side of the road, heading for the bus depot in Santa Fe, thirty-five miles away. At first there were no coherent thoughts in her mind, only alternating rage and the pleasure of the smooth air along the empty road. She had her bankbook in her pocket and nothing else. There was $50 savings noted in the bankbook, her college fund, an accumulation of relatives' graduation gifts. She had walked almost five full miles in the deepening twilight when her mother found her, pulling the family pickup onto the grassy shoulder ahead of Veronica. That made her want to march past the pickup, eyes straight ahead, as if obstacle didn't exist. Mother got out of the truck and came around to the rear, standing in the way and foiling her avenue of defiance. Veronica wouldn't, couldn't look directly at her, and rage burned its misery into the back of her throat, within her a bitter silent battle between panic and defiance until she thought her bursting heart would explode through her chest.

Mother pointed a finger and told her flatly, "Get in the truck. You have to come back now. We can't have this, none of this. Do you hear me? When you get old enough, I will wash my hands of you. Until then we are responsible for you. Stop crying and pay attention. You have to stop crying all the time. You have to pull yourself together. Do what I do. I learned this a long time ago. When you pretend everything is fine, after a while it will be all right. You hear me? You think I don't know better? I have to live in that house too."

When Veronica followed her mother through the kitchen door, Father rose from his chair by the tv. He had been waiting, simmering and waiting. He yanked her by the hair and whacked her with his knuckles and told her not to do anything stupid and dangerous like that anymore. "You understand me?"

"Not in the face!" Mother cried. "She's too old for this and you know it. She didn't even wash the dishes before she took off."

As the days and weeks passed, eventually silence faded and few words dwindled to neutral comments as a great gray atmosphere grew of pretending that nothing violent had happened between the knotty pine walls. Betty locked herself in her bedroom when she was not at school and Mother and Father threw up their hands in helplessness at Betty's isolation. Then Mother told Veronica to apply for the phone company job and Veronica began to drive her slow circles in and around Santa Fe before returning home habitually at the end of the second half of her split shift, arriving around 10:30 at night. She knew nowhere else to go. Her brain froze cold as granite and her ears rang endlessly. Everything in her life became circular, a deep circular ditch, higher than her reach. Mobius strips fascinated her. She doodled endless eights in margins until the telephone company supervisors admonished her. She was only allowed to write the phone numbers and names for person-to-person and collect calls. No doodling. Handle the station-to-station calls quickly. Neat handwriting. Op-er-der. Your number please. No tangents from circling. No arrows straight into the vast unknown, out of the circling. The unknown appeared only as a void. Veronica had been recaptured.

IV

The bridge job began in late spring. Father stayed all week in the distant town, returning late on Fridays, which Betty re-named Frightday. He left on Sunday afternoons to drive the four hours north to the bridge job near Red River.

During the week the atmosphere in the H house became as palatable as springtime.

Jingo leaped when Veronica returned from work each evening. It was too dark to release him from the chain that late. It was forbidden. However, the household was bedded down for the night. Father was far away and reprimands were unlikely. Defiantly she unhooked the chain, grasped a handhold on his hard leather collar, and walked Jingo to the back of the property. Coyotes yipped in the distance and blue moon shadows colored the soft land. There she released him and he ran like a rocket while she gazed at the starry climes of night. The Milky Way enraptured her with its vast expanse. She'd never seen a sky so large, so clear, so full. The night air felt silky smooth. She breathed easily. Sometimes she sat on the ground to look at the stars. Not often, though, because it upset Jingo and he would lick her face and nudge her hands.

On the night of a full moon, crisp and bright, she walked quite a ways with Jingo across the open back country toward Santa Domingo Pueblo. The weather was too cold for snakes, too beautiful for sadness. The piñon rose intermittently in large dark clumps, sometimes taller than Veronica, wide, bushy, not very much taller and never looming. This was truly another world, a world without elms, birches, oaks, those lovely, deep green foliage woods of New England.

She peered into the strange atmosphere of midnight at full moon in the high country of northern New Mexico and never felt alone. Instead this odd moonbathing and stargazing encouraged her and she became infused with a healing wonderment, a bright kind of joy, mysterious and comforting. She began to perceive creatures in the night. There were bats and jackrabbits. Coyotes. Mice. Horses. Cows. Deer. And Jingo who raced without barking, running long arcs away from Veronica and back to her and sometimes around her. He sniffed everything and sometimes he stood icily still on small hillocks, observing, his ears upright. And when fatigue and sleepiness overtook her curiosity, she returned to the house, Jingo following. With great care for silence, she made him a surreptitious extra meal and placed it inside his coop. She reluctantly re-chained him. The cold metal of the snap hook on his collar stung her hand like an icicle.

"Why are you so late?" came her mother's voice from the bedroom.

She spoke the truth, pausing at her own bedroom door and speaking over her shoulder. "I went for a walk with Jingo."

"You're nuts. Go to sleep."

Her bedroom seemed cold and alien, and all its contents -- a bed, lamp, closet, shelves --- belonged to a stranger.

The next morning she arose and following the familiar tick of habit went to work. This continued until she was told to begin again to save her paychecks for college tuition. The following January Veronica began driving a two hour trip daily to university classes in Albuquerque. Leaving at 5:15 a.m. she managed a full schedule of general courses. During the summer she returned to working at the phone company and by the next September she had saved enough money to afford a studio apartment near the university. The apartment was located off Central Avenue in a university neighborhood, along a broad aspen-lined street. She walked for the joy of exploring, crossing nearby streets named Lead, Coal and Silver, admiring the slant of sunlight, green leaves, and homes colored in ice cream colors of pistachio, raspberry, vanilla and mocha. Everything pulled her forward.

There was so much to learn about keeping an apartment. She had to learn how to budget money and buy clothes and shoes and food. She had never, at 19, done these things by herself. Within the week she boldly went into the grocery store and selected ice cream and Wheatena cooked cereal, Tang, bread, raspberry jam, peanut butter, apples, carrots and ginger ale. These were the foods she liked and these became her weekly grocery purchase. Easy as that. Her life expanded slowly. Between her basic, freshman-level classes, she studied. And she explored the campus, built of cement and landscaped with New England-style trees, full of acid-smelling science buildings, tall dorms, art galleries, an enormous library, running tracks, an altogether inviting world. One afternoon she had a happy surprise when she recognized one of her Santo Domingo acquaintances, a sophomore television arts major, and they hung out for a while watching Joan Baez, Ira Sandperl and Dave Harris speak against the Viet Nam War outside the Student Union Building. It was very 60s; make love not war, plop daisies inside gun barrels. Try, try, try to give peace a chance.

On Thanksgiving weekend Veronica drove home early in the morning. She parked, opened the car door, heard little. Coming up to the house, she walked past an empty dog coop, the chain lying in a light dusting of early snow.

The bells rang out their sharp jangle as she opened the door.

"You're back," Mother said flatly.

Father sat in his tv chair. "Look what the wind blew in."

Betty looked up from the where she had been flipping through a teen fashion magazine. One wrist was in a cast. "Good," she declared sullenly, "now that you're here you can cook. I sure don't want to." She rose and headed for her bedroom.

"Where's Jingo?" Veronica spoke to her retreating back. "And what happened to you?"

"The turkey is in the oven," Mother declared as she added more Kahlua to her coffee. "You can do the rest. I could use a break."

Veronica repeated her questions.

"That dog kept jumping through the open windows of cars," Mother responded with an upward jerk of her hands, ignoring the question about Betty's cast. "Anyone who came to the antique shop, Jingo would jump inside their car if they left the windows down. He ate a loaf of bread some people bought at a fancy bakery in Santa Fe. They had their groceries in the back seat. They should have put them in the trunk. I had to give them our bread. That dog went crazy. We can't have that. We're trying to run a business."

"Who were they?" Veronica pleaded. "Where do they live?"

"I think it was the people with the red car." She looked at Father, "Didn't we decide that it was them?"

"I told your sister never to let him loose," Father scowled. "It's your fault. You got him running. That's not good for a dog."

"Don't act like you don't know what we mean. When you were gone, Betty started letting him loose. You're a bad example to your sister. You should be ashamed of yourself. She talks back."

Father interrupted, pointing his finger. "First you, then her."

Mother looked away. "They were arguing. It was an accident. That's all."

"The two of ya's are worthless. Both of you. Never do what you're told. Pieces of shit, you deserve what you get," Father shouted. "Now shut up about it."

"You spoiled that dog!" her mother retorted in a whisper. "You should have never let him loose and now he's gone. End of story."

"I just took him to get ice cream."

Her mother relented, "They came for antiques. Afterward they came inside. I gave them coffee." She turned with questioning innocence to Father who remained enthroned at the table with his arms crossed. "The ones who bought the butter churn, right? Yeah, it was them because we figured out that we never saw that dog after they left. He was around up to then. A young couple. They bought the large butter churn we got in Vermont that time, remember? And a sconce."

"Where do they live?"

"How would I know?"

"Did they write you a check?"

"I never take checks. Cash only."

Veronica yanked open the kitchen door and went outside to Jingo's coop. She stood, flushed and silently raging in the freezing cold air. The tar paper on the dog house was torn in places. The ragged piece of carpet covering the doorway had half-fallen. The mud-caked steel chain beside the coop lay on the bricks among small chunks of hail. She looked across the high open country toward Santa Fe, at the land, the sky, the foothills, searching for a moving dark dog. All the way to the

Sangre de Cristos the sky was roiling and moving swiftly, full of dark snow-burdened clouds.

In the other direction, southwestward, toward Albuquerque and the university, across the enormously wide sky of the American West sunlight broke through clouds and beamed golden over the Rio Grande Valley. The horizon beckoned. Veronica glanced back through the window at the hollow scene inside the house with a mixture of sadness, anger and longing, and the awful recognition of what is not right, not fair, not tolerable, the temporarily obligatory world of family. The cold made her face, hands and ankles ache.

She opened the door and went inside to prepare their meal, and to count hours until she went back to school.

~~ The End ~~

This Is A Remember When Story

Remember when we rode out on horseback over to Viola's ranch to get a Christmas tree? It was barely sunrise and bitter cold. The snow on the ground had a glaze of rime ice. No, not lime. Rime, Dad. Margaritas, aren't you funny thinking of margaritas while hooked up to an IV. Yes, it would be interesting to juice it up but the nurse might notice. Lie back and I'll tell you the story just like we were there again. Remember for Viola that it was always whiskey straight and she would take no other liquor except for maybe rum in a Christmas cake. Yes, or a margarita after a few shots. That's right! Barely sunrise and bitter cold when we went out to get that Christmas tree. Out the backdoor and up to the barn we could hear our boots crunching through the crusty snow. Cold silence. Our footsteps made ripples in a lake of cold silence.

Dawn spread rosy-fingers across the sky and we were rosy-nosed when the cold bit our skin. The sun was slow to come up over the Sangre de Cristos by Santa Fe. We hurried, bent inward, hands in pockets and shivering. How we had longed for sun to warm our shoulders the day before while we patched the turkey pen roof before going in to supper. Cold all day and snow in the night. This morning on the way to the barn the sun gave a giant glint and we stopped to watch the splendid sunrise. A couple of frozen moments in a state of solar awe was all we could endure and you said real low, like always, "Let's git to gittin'."

We aimed to saddle up and continue directly to Viola's ranch. In the light of full sunrise, the horses began stamping and snorting, and their noise broke the thick middle quiet of the air. Over by the cottonwoods some birds began to call out to each other in their manner: *food ... light ... where are you?* and other birds answered. We heard the horses speaking to each other, also. *They're coming ... today they may put molasses in the oats to lure us to the saddle ... it's cold.*

Three horses, two chestnut and one black as tar, wore their thick winter coats; and around their jaws grew single long grey hairs, winter beards which lent them the appearance of huge wizened elves. We placed our hands on their warm sides and necks. We laid our faces against their dusty fur and spoke their names. We felt their warm flesh and their steady breathing. We inhaled their scent and a wonderfully good dusty sweat smell enveloped us until our breathing matched that of the horses. Their great size, their thick, breathing enormity overtook us and once again, at winter sunrise, a special kind of wonder filled our minds with a certain sensation that quiets a person deep inside.

The day began. We tucked the foil-wrapped rum cake and loaves of homemade bread for Viola into the saddle bags. That was my bread recipe with wheat germ and soy flour and powdered milk mixed in with the wheat flour. The loaves always rose high, because we were at nearly 8,000 feet, and smelled so sweet and good. We had breakfast sandwiches in our pockets, fried egg on thick slabs of fresh bread, wrapped in wax paper. At the barn we checked the saddling for each other, each saddle blanket well-placed and neat, no creases, a finger under the belly strap, not too tight on the exhale, the horn of the saddle placed just so behind the withers. We got on and rode three, four miles between Galisteo and Cerrillos,

This Is A Remember When Story

across fairly flat country with slight dips and a few arroyos. We aimed for Viola's Diamond Bend Ranch, in sight of the Ortiz Mountains where the naked dirt tailings of no-go mines pockmarked various hills and the highest peak matched the Sangre de Cristos at 8,140 feet. You pointed out where a roll and a dip here and there among the foothills of the Ortiz resembled the body and head of reclining figures, sleepy giants, sky gazers all. We were lucky to notice. It was so cold my eyeballs felt frozen. The horses went right into it, nose first, steady, no hurry.

No matter, it was good riding. I got down several times to release barbed-wire gates and shut them back up after you went through with the horses, the last one was to the side of a cattle guard on a dirt road. After a while we came upon ten head of cattle eating bright green slabs of fresh hay in their mangers. The alfalfa smell was sharp and green. Around the cattle the snow lay in large, bright patches, interspersed with mud like big white dots among the tossed squares of green hay and trampling brown cattle. High above, clouds were moving swiftly across a blue sky. I wouldn't stare so hard again to watch the movements of clouds moving fast across a broad sky, until years later on Waldron Island in Puget Sound when I was pregnant and living in a little logging camp and saw white clouds passing swiftly through the blue above the Douglas fir treetops and thought of New Mexico skies, and again thirty years later in Ireland with that North Sea sky of constant changing weather. Fast moving clouds then made me nostalgic for home; and now it means the passing of time. It was a long time ago we did this, Dad, that we went to get a Christmas tree and rode out grand at sunrise and trampled in the snow. Grand, that's the word, isn't it or maybe not because we were small and quiet against the big picture that morning, the rosy sunrise, the clouds, the smell of alfalfa.

There we were with the cattle munching their green. You decided we should follow the two tire tracks leading to the ranch house. It was a bit of a ride before we inhaled piñon smoke. We were close.

~:~~:~~:~~:~~:~~:~~:~~:~~:~~:~~:~~:~~:~~ This Is A Remember When Story

As soon as we saw them, the windows of her ranch house trembled warm, reached out and begged us to hurry inside. The adobe walls of her house seemed to be sinking back into the earth. The corners were like tent tarps flung out to hang loosely instead of sharp straight lines --- and her roof, that sad roof, slumped and damp in places. We saw it because we had been working on patching roofs all week, our house, the barn, the turkey pen. We counted how many shingles had blown off Viola's roof and we agreed to tend to it the next day if it didn't snow again and in case we had to go into town to buy shingles although maybe she have some in the barn and that would save us the trip. We muttered only a few words about these roof matters while trotting up to the house.

We tied our horses to the wood rail hitching post near where Viola had parked her battered pickup. The tires were dappled orange with caleche and there were sprays of mud on the white doors, speckled like chicken eggs. Viola waved a come-in from the kitchen window. Behind us, much whinnying, head-tossing and bragging about their sunrise meander ensued as our garrulous horses struck up conversations with the Diamond Bend horses in a nearby corral. We stamped our feet on the welcome mat on the side porch and opened the kitchen door ourselves without knocking. Her kitchen warmth washed over us like a sweet tsunami and all smelled of wood smoke and boiling coffee. I liked the smell and there was a bit of soap in the air as well. A few pieces of laundry hung to dry on a short line above the stove.

We hugged each other, "Merry Christmas!" And I ran back to get the cake and bread from the saddle bags.

"Sit ye down here an' get warmed up," she told us while jovially accepting our gifts. We settled around the kitchen table while she puttered. "I'll pour ye coffee. Gotta take it black 'cause I ran outta canned milk. Hey, at my age, 82 this past August, I skip the milk sometimes, watching my collie-esterol, you know. Careful with that tin cup, the handle gets hot. Here! Here! I want you both to eat a bowl of good green chile to stoke you up. Pack it down. You need it. It's gonna be a far ride for ye Christmas tree."

You asked her to ride with us.

"I won't have a whole tree, not any more," she declared, "I just do with gettin' a nice branch in my Christmas vase. Here's the vase, see," she turned to point to the counter. "That's the bottom of my mama's butter churn. I'll poke a branch in there with some dirt, and I'll string up popcorn outside for the birds. I remember doing that with miner kids in Madrid up the mountain one Christmas. We had no snow a'tall that year and it was an easy ride on horses there and back in the night, no slippery mud. I had to carry a casserole wrapped in a blanket while I rode and there were great stars that night, shooting stars, lots of them, hundreds."

I couldn't discern which was better, to sit at her kitchen table and eat green chile and listen to her stories or ride beside Viola across the land. I suppose riding, still hard to choose. She was living here as a teenager before cars, a ranch wife before jet planes, a widow before town changed so much they had to post speed limits on the highway. The ranchers and the miners always had lots of parties, do-togethers, and visits that made for fine stories that she would spill out like opening a tin can full of buttons and beads, all different colors, all interesting.

"I'll ride out wich-ah," she declared again. Her voice gave you a sense of being hugged. "Give me a chance to see what's-what without getting my truck stuck in the soft stuff. I had the man with a bulldozer from Galisteo come and push over some piñons so's I could get a little more grazing surface. When it dries from this snow I'll start seeding. Damn, seed is expensive. He was here day before it snowed. Stopped in at the house first, sittin' where you are now. He's got a big family, all coming home for Christmas. Except for the ones that died. You heard, two sons, Vietnam. He's got the girls and one is gettin' married in the spring. That means grandchildren, which could help him find the good in life again. Sometimes the good in life wants to hide." She heaved a sigh and turned to the window, "hide and seek," she said with a philosophical dip of her head. "Out there those trees are going to be firewood by next month. No, thank you for the offer. My son will help me with the chainsaw when he comes for the holiday weekend, so I would say all in all that Christmas come along at the right time."

"Always does, doesn't it?" I reacted naively, thinking of the calendar.

"No, hon. Sometimes it rushes up and slaps ye on the back." She gave you a deep look and a wink. "Now let's have some whiskey before we ride."

She threw a big yellow and white potholder in the center of the table and plunked down a bottle, half full. She had those really small shot glasses from Juarez made of thick gray-blue glass. You don't see them too much any more. She poured a lick of whiskey for me too, and we cheered to Christmas and then she tried to re-fill our chile bowls. My eyes watered and cool tears ran down my cheeks and I knew that I could not drink the rest of what was in my little gray blue glass. You took care of it for me.

Viola proceeded to let us know her strong opinions on how to make good chile. "I never put beans in chile. Never liked it that way though some do and I suppose that's their preference. I take my beans plain. Without beans is how my father made chile and that's how my mother insisted he keep on makin' it. Just roasted green chiles, and I mean fresh roasted and peeled, and beef and well yes, I do add some cumin seed to give a reminder of springtime 'cause cumin has the aroma of flowers. And a dot a honey."

She had a sweet voice, clear, strong and feminine. Viola was a skinny woman who always wore western clothes, basic denim boot-cut jeans, a black leather belt with her name carved along its backside, a fine silver buckle holding a roughly polished hunk of turquoise, a long sleeved shirt with pearly snap buttons and a puffy down vest. Her eyes were pale and she had a direct gaze. Her hair was braided and pinned around her head, German style. She fussed over us and we liked it very much. "Now here, lemme put some whiskey in your coffee or you'll get whiskers like the horse

This Is A Remember When Story

out there in the cold. Yes, you do need it. Looky," she stretched to read the thermometer outside the window. "It's 25 degrees out there. In the sun! That's too cold for an empty stomach. I aim to get ye warmed all the way though."

"You know what that will take," you flirted with her.

"I'm never too old for that fun stuff but I am alive enough that your wife would shoot me." She laughed and you laughed and both thought I was too young to get it completely.

"I been out there this morning," she told us. "I gave my cattle a little feed to tide them over until the snow is gone. If the sun shines warm by tomorrow, that snow should melt completely."

Then we fell to chattering like birds in the morning and explaining stuff and telling tales of wonderment and elaborating on how best to fix a windmill and how often to clean a water tank and the controversy of what makes the best fruitcake no fruit or more pecans and that the last governor was a rancher before he had to go live in the capitol and listen day after day to complaints instead of cattle talk and horse talk. We got onto the if & how everyone could one day form a cooperative fire station in Cerrillos.

"We can do it," she encouraged us since we were newbies to the area, "there's no some day, there's only now. There's a need. Ye think ye know how to fill it. Then it must get done. The best way is when people do it together and share in it, and not wait for the someone an hour away who ye have to call and they may not be home if ye want 'em to bring their water truck when your house is on fire." She leaned over and grinned at me and told me to remember the best way because, "the other way is when you have to do it by yourself and that's really hard. Ye got to concede sometimes, give up on doin' it purely yer own way just so's it gets done and finished."

At that point you slapped the table and said, "Let's git to gittin'."

We all happily agreed. Viola got her sheepskin jacket and gloves, checked that the stove was turned off, the fire banked,

~:~~:~~:~~:~~:~~:~~:~~:~~:~~:~~:~~:~~:~~:~~ *This Is A Remember When Story*

and her cat had food. She handed me a few pieces of carrot for our horses. Outside we watched her saddle Old Sabino, a 20 hand chestnut and white beauty who responded to her Athena touch as if together they were complete. We got up on our horses and left the warm house far behind, riding away steadily, not too fast not too slow, toward the southeast and across her ranch, toward a broad swath of land beyond the horizon, the light blue Ortiz Mountains always in our sights.

She led us down one arroyo, special to her, pointing out water-cuts that exposed pottery and folded woven mats from people who were here long before the ranch, before the Santo Domingo village, before even their beginnings, perhaps the Anasazi people. She told us not to touch it or ride too close because the university was coming to study it. We rode up out of the arroyo's soft sand onto a plain, where we spotted a couple of criss-crossing jackrabbits, some sweet chirpers in the bush, and a pale coyote with eyes of steel who crossed in front of us as if he were holding the speed limit on the interstate, cruise control. She didn't like him. We could tell by the way she made throat sounds as if his appearance was noted. Finally we reached higher yet flat acreage where our Christmas trees were dotting her newly acquired graze land. They all lay on their sides and I was dismayed at the awful sight. Green bushy trees knocked over. I had never seen anything so strange. I dismounted and touched their short trunks, rounded crowns and short needles. A few pinyon jays dashed about in the vicinity, screaming their *Ike, Ike* like they were looking for a past president.

Me, me, each tree pleaded in the chorus. *I'm bigger. I'm fuller. My needles are green and thick and my trunk is straight.*

You and Viola dismounted and walked around the offerings, holding the reins loosely, surveying each tree in the crisp and clean air. Truth be told and I could not state it then, but there was a sadness to see the bushy trees lying there on their sides, about a hundred pulled out and pushed over, their roots standing on end like huge dark, filigree disks filled with dirt and light colored rocks. A yellow bulldozer was parked near the barbed wire fence, a steel cable attached to its rear, thick and loop-ended. The earth was churned back and forth criss-cross by its tracks.

"He's nearly finished by the looks and I won't have him do any more," she declared with a long face. "Makes me ache but ye do what ye have t'do. Though trees are scarce enough, I need the grass." She shook her head slowly. "Well, go on and pick out the one ye want. Get a nice one."

We walked around more fallen trees and stared at their root disks and width of bushiness. The conversation drifted to cattle. You asked, "Viola, how many head will you send to market this year?"

"Oh, those days are gone. The carnicero comes and takes them away and he brings the packaged meat to my few buyers. No more cattle drives to the railroad loader, m'dear, I only do for taxes, light bills, and groceries. A new blouse now and then." She smiled at me and turned back to you. "I only do what-for's, now. I sell to a few people in town and who live along the highway. Did ye know they are changing the name of the highway from ten to fourteen? I thought they might give it a nice name this time, like Golden Highway or Turquoise Trail. Well, some day."

Dad, you untied the handsaw. Never said a word about what a bother it had been while riding.

"Did you ever go on a cattle drive?" I asked with anticipation.

"Eighteen," she replied, pursed her lips and shut up.

I ached for more and stood close looking up at her face. She relented. "Each one of those was like the pieces of pottery we saw a ways back. A time passed on into memory. Just a little piece of the whole thing."

"How many cattle would you herd to the railroad?"

"Hundreds. They didn't want to go. Plus they go in circles, ye know, so everyone has to really work hard to get them from A to B. Trucks make a nice difference. When ye got there those damn cows that give so much trouble didn't weigh as much nor was the pay a whole lot. I knew it then and I know it now looking back. No one was rich; we just lived. We had to have the Association."

"Viola was Cattleman of the Year five times," you told me.

"Didn't they change the name?"

"What do you mean, honey?"

"To Cattle Woman."

She laughed and her laugh ended hard. "Like a beauty queen?" I could tell she wanted to say more. "One time they gave me the award I think to stop the bickering between a couple ranchers with big egos and mean mouths. Maybe it was a good thing I was there and contributed to the peace. I do pay attention to my cattle and I grew this ranch. I held on. It'll all go to my son. I don't know fer sure what he'll do with it, hard to say." She twisted in the saddle and waved to you as you wandered this way and that looking for a tree we could handle, not too big and unwieldy. We had to drag it back wrapped in a tarp or get a really small one to carry it in our arms, which we didn't want to do. Dad? Oh I see, you are not asleep, you are just resting your eyes. I could go get coffee. All right, I will stay.

Viola looked over every inch almost of the landscape both close by and far away. She rubbed her eyes and her dry skin wrinkled like a soft cloth. She told us, "My name is on a couple a shiny plaques. Ye can see them in my living room when we get back. Look there. That's where I pulled out their fence posts when I bought these acres. Holes in the ground now. Just remember when some day. Remember when we did make marks on this land, some of it good, some of it ugly, and some of it needs to be put right again."

She spread her arms parallel in one direction, "I told him to stop over there. No, he did too many. He got overkill fever. That's what happened. He caint put them back now, can he?" She sniffed and muttered, "Firewood. More'n I'll ever need at my age."

In the distance we heard the cattle calling to each other, birds flickered nearby, and a jackrabbit ran past, zigzagging in surprise when he noticed us. On the ground where dots of snow melted in the higher rising sun, little things began to glitter, small pieces of quartz, mica, granite, the caleche soil scuffed by our shallow footprints. The sun was high enough to make shadows.

We selected a tree, sawing the roots from its disk, trimming branches. We chopped a fine branch for Viola which had a great bouquet, a roundness of foliage. We fixed up a drag for our third horse.

Once inside our home our own Christmas tree expanded hugely, double its outdoor size, and not really suitable in the opinions of others who had not gone along on the ride. We cut and hacked and trimmed and cut some more. Later in the warmth of our house the tree opened its branches and exuded both a piney smell and an annoying hatching of flies that we dealt with somehow. Nothing is ever sublimely smoothly perfect, not in real life, right Dad? They're here to change the IV again, no, they're going to come back in a few minutes. I'll just keep talking and you can keep your eyes shut.

We did go back to Viola's the next Monday in the truck with the tools and ladder and an opened bundle of our own shingles. We brought those longer nails that are needed on the ridge shingles. We climbed up there and patched her roof and afterward sat in the kitchen again and ate plain beans with tortillas and salsa and admired her decorated branch stuck in the brown pottery bottom of a butter churn. Her branch held shiny glass balls and colorful yarn ojo de dios. She showed us those plaques on her living room wall. Cattleman of the Year. Five times.

That tree was the best tree we ever had. Some lower branches we cut off were used for wreaths and fireplace mantle decorations. Our house filled up with decorations. Strings of blue lights circled our tree. A fire in the fireplace, molasses for the horses, guests at Christmas dinner and a day of peace and understanding, just ordinary unspoken commitments to a day of kindness and a sense that the extraordinary was an ordinary part of being alive. Years passed and Viola died and the Diamond Ranch went to her son. He sold it within two years, as she probably knew he would. The cattle and Old Sabino gone too but getting the

~:~~:~~:~~:~~:~~:~~:~~:~~:~~:~~:~~:~~:~~ This Is A Remember When Story

tree comes back year after year as a great memory, don't you think? And that is how this story became a Remember When story.

~~ The End ~~

THE NORTHWEST

A bird ...

flies through the air and lands in my wading pool. "Landfall!" my uncle screams like a banshee pirate hanging from the yardarm with a telescope pressed to one stark eye. His greasy hair hangs in ringlets. The three of us haven't had a bath in over a week and his wife and I ditched our plans to get into the wading pool in our underwear and do a mani-pedi afterward. During the night a long rain had filled our inflatable toddler pool, the makeshift bathtub for our campsite on this dot of an island far along the Aleutian chain. On a clear day we can see Siberia. Sometimes.

"Shearwaters," he calls out as he heads for the shore. Now all we see are birds, so many they are darkening the sky. Another plummets down and lands panting at my feet, and instantly six more, twenty more, a hundred. Then too many to count, surrounding us in all directions with feathers and noise, yes, far too many to see Russia anymore.

Ned and Adele are excited beyond words. Their body motions slow, their mouths sag, and their eyes bug out. I have

~:~A bird ...

seen this kind of behavior before and I have tagged it The Curiosity Addiction, unique to biology professors. I mean they can squat still forever silently watching an animal. Ned was once clocked at eleven hours watching an eagle sleeping on a tree limb. "He was snoring," Ned told me later, defending himself.

Within minutes the flat rocks behind their battered Airstream is covered with a fallen mass of thousands of bleating, panting, exhausted shearwaters. They have flown from Australia to the Aleutian Islands in a misguided circular quest to eat bugs, I presume, during the Arctic summer. I look across at the sheet of water between here and Russia, where everything looks the same but they speak another language. As I stretch my hand, the width of water in the channel measures the same as the length of my hand. It's a mystery how people live the way they do, speaking different languages. It's like wondering about the neighbors across the street in an imaginary neighborhood where they have many trees in front of their house and you know nothing about them except the name on the mailbox, if there is a name on the mailbox.

My uncle is a dedicated scientist, and I suppose I could be too, but I like music and Thai food better than the loneliness of a wildlife observer. I thought that I would like it. I did agree to come. No not really. I gave in. This was a plan my parents created for me "before she gets into real trouble." When I got here, I was told to turn off my cell phone. I didn't know that was going to be part of it.

"Come on," he hiss-yells, "They're Tasmanian shearwaters!"

Adele will inform me later that the true name of a Tasmanian shearwater is Puffinus tenuirostiris and she spells it for me and shows me how to speak Latin by saying each syllable slowly. No accent, a plain language. It's nice done in calligraphy and I'm glad I brought colored pens for something to do after supper every night. Besides, I can get credit for this at my high school, and maybe get out of there sooner. Maybe.

~:~ *A bird ...*

Ned gestures with a slight motion of one hand for us to join him as he walks low to the ground, almost to the waters edge, knees buckled, until he is on all fours like a crapping penguin, he's a twerker, and then poom he's prone right in the middle of all those grey and white yellow-beaked squawking blobs of feathers. The birds smell peculiar like dusty blood. Must be their sweat.

Adele imitates Ned and gets to the ground. She is soft and quiet and gets even more relaxed when she is dirt-challenged. These two are my Relatives of a Different Order. The rest of my family, the ones I live with during the rest of the year because I am in high school and I have to live somewhere, would rather pay money than lie face down on the dirt. It isn't so bad, I want to tell them. I won't. They would pat me on the head.

It is true, however, that I would rather be with my friends or at least texting them. Instead, this is the summer I have to be here and I have no way to get off this hump of rock and there is nothing else to do but assist the research and Simple Simon my uncle every knee buckling step, until I am also just like Ned and Adele, flat on my stomach, peering at these exhausted birds. I can see their bird heart beats pushing their breasts in and out, fast. Some of the birds' heads are lolling to one side. There are thousands and they are too tired to be afraid of us. "Be a rock," my uncle whispers, "move slowly."

We do a sloth crawl when the body gets stiff from stillness. I like pretending to be a flat rock, a little skimmer that can almost float. I like the shearwaters. There is something weird and tender about them, something all about being alive, about being a tiny creature with amazing endurance. About flapping wings for ten thousand miles and getting there at last and landing and saying to each other Shit We Made It Ahrrrr. I want to shiver a little and celebrate with them. I want the birds to see me smile at them. I want to know their language. A sound comes out of my throat, a very tiny squawking sound. Imitating two birds nearest my face I squawk three tiny bleats in a row. One replies, kind of. I really think he answered me and that is so astonishing that I can

~:~ *A bird ...*

only describe it as feeling clean and being happy and full of sunlight. My three squawky bleats say 'I can smell the wet dark rocks and not-at-all-soft lichen in my nose', the smell of fishy stuff and seaweed and the wet sand and the cold sea and bird poop and my own funk all mixing together. I am saying that my fingers are all red and banged up and my clothes are wet. I am saying that these birds surprised me when they fell out of the sky panting and half full of life and half full of near-death. And they were tired and funny and exhausted and every moment they become much more half-alive than half-dead. That's the diff. I see the lines on their beaks and their eyes and all their little grey and white feathers.

So what if this was the summer that my parents forced me to come up here as punishment for hanging out with some people who turned out to be nasty who lied to me and betrayed me, and for all that my parents made me count birds for my uncle on his special university grant. He took me to an island the size of a dot at the end of nowhere. It wasn't nowhere to these birds who Ned says have a bit more to go after resting up in order to get to a certain river in Siberia. This was turning out to be one of the weirdest mixed-up stinkingest summers I ever had to endure to the point of actually liking what was around me not that I'd tell them about it. It was not a vacation; it was freakin' real. Wow, everyone should be here.

~~ The End ~~

Comet

Not long after their marriage, in early June of 1973, Veronica and Thomas moved to the Pacific Northwest. They packed their few belongings into the back of a pale blue Ford pickup and an egg-shaped aluminum trailer, leaving behind the high desert and purple mountains majesty of Southern California, heading toward a dark green island in Puget Sound, Washington State. Their destination, an place called Orcas Island where Thomas had spent idyllic summers as a child. The live-in trailer was a 1967 Comet, not yet ten years old and painted with two flashy red stripes, wraparound picture windows in the front, white sidewall tires, and a fat propane tank on top of the hitch. The Comet was small and bright and self contained, a wedding gift from Thomas' father, Bob, a laconic, red-headed steel worker in Fontana, California. Bob had been hard-pounded year after year in the Kaiser steel mill, a bitter sweat, split fingers job with pay raises measured in dimes and quarters. Fifteen years into the job Bob had become prone to slowly sucking his teeth before

~:~~:~~:~~:~~:~~:~~:~~:~~:~~:~~:~~:~~:~~:~~:~~:~~:~~:~~:~ Comet

speaking and saying only what needed to be said. The Comet was one in a long series of Bob's trailer purchases trying different sizes and shapes to best outfit his own, secretive dream of long weekends fishing in the Salton Sea.

Thomas grasped the trailer as a means to never again pay rent. He philosophically defined cost-free as the true root of freedom. Veronica nested in the Comet, adoring its womb qualities and oval shape complimentary to her pregnancy. For both, the air tight door and windows sealed out a world that might squeeze hard to make them bitter too, scrunch them up and crush their marriage before their own dreams had a chance to thrive.

On the road Veronica and Thomas sang their freedom anthem, the Woody Guthrie song Ramblin' Boy. But by the third day of travel, coziness and boredom alternated like blacktop and white lines inside the cab of the pickup. Song and conversation wound down to little more than map reading. Thomas sped nearly non-stop toward Orcas, or so Veronica thought, wishing to roam and wander. This disparity brought back old resentments. A marital rift reappeared once they were out of Bob's sight. This sembral crack had begun shortly after the marriage during a dispute --- violent and the first of many --- about money, living quarters, money, laundry, booze, dope, money-money-money. The intent of this journey to Puget Sound was flight, to shake off those invisible beer cans attached by black ribbons to a newlywed bumper. We'll try again somewhere pure, they announced to parents and siblings. A clean break, wipe the slate of repeat-repeat, forget all those arguments. This is our chance. Neither Veronica nor Thomas admitted to each other the sense of doom hitchhiking with them. Each cruelly blamed their own selves for ruining what had been a magical gift of a soft, dreamy love affair. Neither had an answer for why in their lives all things inevitably turn out wrong after a while. Truth, they had only known each other four months before marrying and so it wasn't that they had grown up or grown apart; more that with deeper knowledge, they now cared less for each other.

On the road their rift alternately opened like a wound and shrank into a touch-sensitive scar. Their conversations stultified. Veronica began to hold her body always tilted slightly away from Thomas and looking out the passenger window rather than the front window, silently recognizing a growing sense of panic in her throat below her voice box. She had to stay. She was pregnant and scared of being alone. Unspoken thoughts about the future swung back and forth with foreboding and optimism. As they sped past Santa Rosa, Mount Shasta, Bend, Tacoma, her hand sometimes grazed the door handle, cool, metallic, hard, all the opposite of what lay beneath her skin, an internal roiling of insecurity, hormones, screechy clinginess. Thomas pushed toward the summers of peace he had known as a child, the comfort and freedom of a child loved by grandparents. He hated the gas station bathrooms, highway rest stops, watery coffee, faces of strangers, the whining wife, and wanted only the blur of speed. Thomas and Veronica rode a forward momentum dragged to ground level by dark thoughts, released to the airborne by any odd new highway sight. Their troubles were hitched to the bumper of their marriage; their comet would be brief, full of stars and dust and hope. And a baby.

After a week of uneven sleep in rest stops while parked between diesel trucks with idling engines, they caught the last ferry from Anacortes, nearly the last vehicle to board. Floating across Puget Sound with the pickup and trailer on the ferry's lower deck, their misgivings and fatigue began to dissipate; after all, the end was near and their idyll was about to begin. Bring on the banjos. Things are looking up.

The ferry arrived on Orcas Island long after sunset. The ferry unloading was full of the noise of metal wrench and ship thumps against pilings. All the other vehicles zipped away on invisible pathways nevermore to be seen, or so it felt. Thomas drove across a silent island on unlit roads with dense woods on both sides of the road, scarcely another vehicle in sight, a few lights from homes visible from the road. He turned left in the immense dark at a mile point that, to Veronica's perception, was illuminated briefly in the headlights like a religious apparition. She understood suddenly and woefully the saying that hope is a candle flame.

Thomas humped the pickup along a rutted road through the woods for about two or three lonely miles, with Veronica wincing on each bump. She kept her face turned away, not letting him see her distress. He sensed her distress nonetheless and did not know what to say or do besides lower the gears and ease over the washboard corners. It was hard to slow down, for once the ferry left the docks back at Anacortes, he had become strangely excited, all jumpy and crazy inside with a happiness that he hadn't felt since he was ten years old. He had forgotten such glee remained inside him --- squelched while concentrating on acting as he thought a husband should act, watchful, silent, and appearing in control despite confusion or ignorance. All that pretense was left behind at the docks. Now a silly grin lit up his face in the glow of the dashboard.

At last he stopped the pickup at an entrance to a long driveway filled with many vehicles parked every which way. Veronica rolled down her window and inhaled cold, wet night air. There were vertical streaks in the night, darker than the dark --- these were huge trees. Enormous, thick pine trees stood so close to the pickup that she could reach her hand through the window and nearly touch the bark. She could smell the wet soil and musty hardwoods, and taste a night air filled with their dense coolness. It was complex and very different from the desert of Southern California.

Shrieks pierced the night, coming from the deck of a brightly lit cabin that glinted between the trees. She heard yelling, drunken yelling --- Class of 73 --- We Made It --- Goodbye High School --- teenagers celebrating with a graduation kegger. After the yelling receded to hoots and erratic loud music, she turned her attention to the massive presence of dense forest on both sides of the road. The woods were deep and dark and absorbingly thick. An unexplainable, irregular groaning issued erratically from the forest. As she listened more closely, the groans increased. She shrunk back into her seat, fearful, but saying nothing.

"Big trees creak all the time," Thomas reassured her. "They make that noise when they lean and sway in the wind."

He could always read her moods, sometimes better than she could. She believed that he understood people better than she could, and that was a quality in Thomas that she admired greatly. Her own objectivity was unfocused; as if lens after lens snapped into place to thicken glasses --- one way to describe impairment stemming from an irregular childhood --- and both of them had some kind of inherent attachment disorder or bonding irregularity or relationship mayhem --- lenses again snapped thickly in place until perception became distorted and cloudy judgment became habitual. People, their thoughts and feelings, were a constant mystery to Veronica, who considered most people unpredictable and the world unsafe. She lived isolated in a solemn internal place. Her father-in-law told her --- and she believed it --- that she was too shy and too quiet and lived too much in her mind. She did not understand what 'lived too much in her mind' meant. Her reaction to the unknown was to smile and turn away in embarrassment, to hide. She liked quietude, books and soft music. Quite the contrary, with others Thomas was amiable and easygoing and celebratory, the kind of person that strangers felt comfortable with immediately. He was happiest in a gathering where he would lose himself in glee and revelry. When the party was over then a bit of sour glumness set in.

"Those are douglas fir mostly on this part of the island," he spoke again, trying to regain her attention. The pickup was cooling inside now that the engine was turned off and the windows rolled down so they could both smell the night air. "Practically virgin forest. Never been logged since the last century. Four arms around, maybe more. Probably some hemlock and madrona, too. I'll show you the differences in the daylight. You'll soon learn to tell one from the other."

Discovery of new things, the types and names of trees, fish, birds, all part of the promise that had pulled them into this journey. A promise of fresh discovery, that was the reminder of why they had traveled so far. The sound of his voice with its melodic timbre restored her confidence. By the light of the dashboard she secretly studied Thomas' profile and the rise of his fine, blonde hair . Looking at his handsome features was part of being in love, a feathery part that she wished she could hold onto longer, keep it, feel it like a smooth rock in her pocket, like a true dream. His mere presence as her husband, her idealized protector, her partner, should dissipate her fear. This she believed in a naive, almost primitive manner, idealizing marriage far beyond its complicated reality. Her simplistic expectation was that if her brain froze in fear at the strangeness of anything at all, these threats would shrink in the presence of her prince.

 The dome light went on when Thomas opened the driver's door. As he pulled on a plaid wool jacket, she reminded herself that he had lots of family here. This was a small island with not many roads and there were lots of people who knew Thomas. She knew the southwest desert where trees grew to the size of bushes and there was plenty of ground space between for sand and rocks. Was the ground here too wet to hold these massive evergreens upright? Would they fall over? Fall on top of the pickup? Were the trees talking? Were they angry? Did they dislike strangers? Random, arrhythmic bursts of creak discharged from all sectors of the surrounding woods as if malevolent spirits were inside and abusing the tall hulks, or if tree spirits were beating to get out. Veronica felt a stranger in a dark place where fairy tales from the Black Forest turned out to be really grimly true.

 Thomas doubled back and kissed her through the open passenger-side window. "There's nothing to worry about. I'll go find my cousin inside and he'll give us directions to Grandpa's new place. He just graduated from high school this year. He'll be in there."

 Thomas would never stay with her if there was a party he could get to. She rubbed her hands lightly on her belly, rounded with baby. She was awfully tired. Think good thoughts, she commanded herself. Hormones are keeping you scared like a chicken. Don't let your imagination take over all the time. Keep it for the songs you write. Sing a sweet song in your mind for the baby, a lullaby to calm yourself. She rolled up the window hard and buttoned her coat snugly, pulling her hands inside the sleeves.

The pickup got thoroughly cold before Thomas returned, crashing noisily down a ditch trail beside the driveway. He smelled sharply of beer. He wanted her to come inside and meet some people. Though chilled, she agreed and went up the driveway following Thomas, straining her eyes to adjust to the path. She pushed back large, whipping ferns and her pants got soaked by low rhododendron branches.

She stepped up to the big wooden deck and into the crowd of the party. Immediately she lost Thomas in a sea of strangers who all seemed to know each other. She moved forward in and around people and squeezed through the doorway into a brightly lit house without furniture and full of party. There must have been one hundred teenagers there. No one knew her. Everyone seemed nearly ten years younger. No one wanted to meet her eyes. Teenagers were leaning, talking, dancing, screeching, weaving, puking, and slopping plastic cups of beer. No one seemed to be able to speak coherently. Again, she shrunk within herself and kept a small smile on her face. Two girls who looked fourteen asked her to go with them to buy some wine. Others glanced inquiringly at her pregnant belly and just as quickly looked away.

The crowd was thinner in the kitchen. She looked through the window above the sink out onto the deck where a large aluminum barrel of beer and its upright, stick pump held regal position surrounded by drinkers. Suddenly Thomas appeared, coming toward her with two large cups of beer. She felt hot and clammy and nauseous, overwhelmed. She didn't want the beer. She wanted to leave and Thomas did not. He kept introducing her to young men whose skin was pimply and eyes were reddened, heavy-lidded or wet. Sometimes their hands clasped hers in soft, weak handshakes. She couldn't remember which face belonged to his cousin. She was road-tired and a somewhat dizzy from driving eighteen hours straight before reaching the ferry. She longed to wrap herself in a wool blanket and eat a hot bowl of soup and go to sleep. She lost Thomas as the jubilant crowd surged outside to the deck where a fiddler was playing bluegrass tunes. A banjo player joined the fiddler, and a mandolin player, and the delighted crowd whooped. Suddenly she spied Thomas, dancing by himself to the music, howling and weaving crazily. Cripple Creek, Darling Corey, Foggy Mountain Breakdown. Faster and faster in swirls of noise and twirls of color. Beyond the deck, the groaning woods deepened in black pitch. There was no relief. She stood invisible in a turbulent sea of strangers.

Veronica struggled through the crowd to the door, carefully stepped around the crazily parked vehicles in the driveway and slipped past the frightening groans in the woods. She unlocked the door of their little trailer, tugged it open and swam inside to its sanctuary. When the Comet's door shut snugly, she was safe, cold but safe. Her hand rested on the smooth wall paneling of honey-colored wood. She went past the self-contained kitchen with overhead storage cabinets, tiny sink, small refrigerator, small oven and a small two-burner stove. Small was the operative word for everything within the trailer. Veronica crawled onto the cozy bed in the rear, fully clothed, pushed off her shoes, pulled two heavy quilts over her head, and fell into a deep sleep within minutes. The treetops bent over her in dreams of walking in a gossamer dress beside large, striped animals.

By noon the next day Thomas maneuvered the Comet into the driveway beside Grandpa's long silver and turquoise trailer in the Rosario Resort Employees Trailer Village. Grandpa had been waiting for them since yesterday, expecting them to set up in his driveway as a temporary location until they could establish themselves with job and home and get rooted.

Grandpa was 86, and his second career --- begun after selling the farm in a divorce --- had been as chief gardener for the resort. Retired since the age of 75, the resort allowed him to live rent-free in the Trailer Village, a ten-acre tract that had been slash-logged. There were electric and water hookups and four other trailers plus a few RVs, with wide spaces between each, and woods surrounding on three sides. Grandpa's life revolved around his small garden, family and church. Two decades later employees would be on their own to seek housing and the tree-cleared tract would be developed into six luxury cabins with vast redwood decks and two-story atriums; but for now the Trailer Village was quiet and bright, with trails through the surrounding woods leading to a nearby lake in Moran State Park.

Thomas immediately regained familiarity with every trail in the state park. He came back one day full of energy from an unexpected discovery. He convinced Veronica to return with him to the remote Twin Lakes, halfway up the mountain inside the state park. Leaving the road, they hiked an overgrown trail to a large madrona tree with peeling burgundy park and exposed pale bark. His initials marked that tree at the seven foot high level, there since he had been eight years old, moving upward with growth every year. Memories returned to him from the summers he had been sent to the northwest. This was pure freedom for a kid," he explained. "I could run loose on my own, fishing and hiking and exploring all day until suppertime."

She watched his face as he spoke even though he had cast his eyes downward in thought; and as sometimes happens between those who love each other, there she witnessed the release that his regained memories gave him, a bright cloth of joy wiped away the dust of confusion and left a trail of sparkling motes in the air around him.

He led her past the tree through the brush to his favorite place to go fishing, a small, still pond. Occasional tiny bubbles burst on the surface from bass and trout, snatching May flies and other insects. There was no sound of car engines, traffic, airplanes, chain saws, voices. Only expanding depth, soft to the ears and infinite with calm. Standing close together, still as rocks and not speaking, they watched a deer enter the pond and swim across. A startling burst of loud drilling from a woodpecker drew their gazes upward. A dark bird the size of a crow, with a red flash on his forelock, studiously hammered his beak through thick tree bark to capture a mysterious savory treat. Small brown sparrows with black stripes on their heads ran along the forest floor, seeking seeds. A bird with white tail feathers swooped past them. Thomas broke off a fiddle head fern with a tightly coiled top piece and handed it to her like a royal scepter. This was their first day, the real first day on the island, and Veronica made note where real time began. As they walked back to the Comet, they fell into slow and easy conversation on their plans for the next few weeks, to find an inexpensive rental cabin, a job for Thomas, a crib for the baby. They made dreams ---a large family, a small farm, a wood burning cookstove, two cats, two dogs, a cow and Rhode Island Red chickens, and maybe a small skiff for catching salmon.

When a few weeks had passed, the creaking of the trees receded to background sounds. Veronica could name a few tall trees and identify the sound of a drilling woodpecker, a couple varieties of rhododendrons; she tried recipes using fiddlehead ferns and picked blackberries.

They lived rent free while Thomas looked for a job. The job hunt took time because it was not an easy task in the rural, depressed economy. They secretly tallied their dwindling cash reserves. They would not starve; yet how would they thrive? At low tides they learned to dig clams for chowder dinners. The uncles invited them to go salmon and cod fishing. And Veronica assisted Grandpa by driving him to doctor appointments and errand-related excursions, settling into a fairly sedentary life as her pregnancy progressed. Thomas never once yielded to a sense of urgency. Each morning Veronica's greatest unspoken mission was to imitate Thomas' relaxed attitude. Terrible headaches assailed her and she took mid-afternoon naps to get relief.

Veronica made jam from the wild blackberries. She grew to know Thomas' grandfather, who encouraged her to can clams. She mastered a recipe for pickled salmon with onions and spices. She learned to bake bread. While she kneaded the dough, she listened to Grandpa's stories of the olden days when he had been a homesteader, circa 1905.

~:~*Comet*

Some mornings while Thomas was out job hunting and the bread dough was rising, she and Grandpa drove to odd sectors of the woods behind the state park, along old logging roads. They went to seek the abandoned, overgrown homesteads of island history. She located many homesteader garbage dumps and retrieved old blue canning jars to use for flower vases. At these abandoned and decaying homesteads, Grandpa sat in the car with the passenger side door wide open, tired old feet placed on the ground, leaning on his cane, breathing the air of the woods and reminiscing. He told about each homesteader family, how like his own or unlike, how one grew only pears and another only peas, or how they kept pigs or chickens, or planted acres of fruit orchards, apples, plums, raspberries, all produce for sale to the mainland. Veronica listened carefully to his rendition of all the possible reasons why one homesteader succeeded and another failed, a reasoning, Grandpa explained as sometimes easy to recall now that seventy years had passed -- the well ran dry, a tree fell on the man and killed him, the work was too hard for the inexperienced and/or lazy, the wife ran off, there was a dire sickness, the boat sank -- adventurous human nature wearied by travail.

While Grandpa told these stories, Veronica listened and rubbed dirt off the blue canning jars to make them shine in the light. Later, in bed, she would re-tell his stories to Thomas. Once after breakfast she watched Thomas through the Comet's windows as he stood outside, examining the blue jars. He was remembering his grandmother, he replied to the question she called out the door, all her shelves of canned vegetables and fruits, dilly beans, blackberry jam, spiced pears, tomatoes, applesauce, apple butter, meat and chopped clams too. Veronica nodded with each item Thomas recalled. She was beginning to understand how much work a homestead demanded.

Grandpa came out of his trailer and went, as his habit, straight to the vegetable garden. He was a large boned, slender man and, like Thomas, gregarious and amiable. Both by nature were inclined to work outdoors. Grandpa was slowed somewhat by age and arthritis. Although he could not dance any longer, he loved to sing the songs of his teenage years. He would sit on a tall stool in the middle of his garden plot and reach with an extended hoe to weed in a circle around him. Plants liked him.

Although Veronica worried silently about finances and where they would live with the baby due in the fall, she stayed busy baking and canning and helping Grandpa. She learned that unoccupied time fueled her anxiety and fears, but activity filled her thoughts with patience and trust. For a little more than three idyllic months, life alongside Grandpa, who was singularly and simply a good human being, strongly influenced what would become, upon retrospection, the calmest period in the married life of Veronica and Thomas. During those months they did not have a single disagreement. Although uncertainties colored their future, they cared for each other, through the influence of Grandpa, with a gentleness and politeness that seemed to belong to another century.

Finally Thomas got a job. The *finally* ending their discreetly concealed money problem and initiating a sad move away from Grandpa. The work required living on another island. Thomas was offered a job with a logging company, assigned to clean up acreage that had been accidentally logged when property boundaries were mistaken. Part of the settlement between the property owner and the logging company included clearing the debris left behind from slash logging --- ugly torn and broken limbs, exposed half-fallen dead trees and barren stumps. Thomas would have to even out the deeply gouged soil. As he explained it over that night's chowder and cornbread dinner with Grandpa and Veronica, he was hired to make it look like a park so the settlement would hold and the owners would not litigate.

The location was on a remote island, not ferry-served, and without telephone, electricity or stores. There was an airstrip, two small piers, and a weekly mail delivery. It was said that 75 people lived on Waldron Island, although maybe half of that number were summer home people and the remaining, half were fishermen who went away to Alaska for a portion of the year. The island children, less than a dozen, used a two-room schoolhouse. Some rode horses and ponies to school. He made Waldron sound sweet, peaceful, idyllic, like the tv show Walton's Mountain.

They would have to hire his uncle's private amphibian ferry service to bring the pickup truck and Comet across the channel to where the logging company granted them use of a meadow near their proprietary pier on Waldron, a rent-free living space through October when the clearing task was expected to be completed.

At the end of July they celebrated their one year anniversary in the meadow. Their baby girl was expected in early September. They were living like a campfire Adam and Eve. Before bed each night they sat outside the Comet on folding lawn chairs and identified constellations and watched for meteorites streaming into the atmosphere, tracing small arcs and making big wishes. Grandpa's quiet guidance --- the impression that he made by example --- plus their time on this remote island in a quiet meadow lifted Veronica and Thomas away from the push and pull of opposing forces; what the world wanted them to do, what they didn't know how to do. Simultaneously their pettiness evaporated and a bit of love magic was regained. They had stumbled at last into an extended honeymoon in a peaceful haven. Nighttime in the meadow, a small aluminum trailer, two lawn chairs and the stars overhead.

"Comets shed the debris that become meteor showers," Thomas read from a astronomy book using a flashlight with a piece of red cloth over its light.

"I didn't know that," Veronica replied slowly, her hands on her belly, gazing upward. "However our lives change in the years to come, please let's remember now forever."

The Perseid meteor showers were especially beautiful that year. All the falling stars spent their quiet fireworks over the small meadow on the small island, burning bright across the dark sky, arcing brief, traceable paths, so brief and wondrous

~:~*Comet*

until time moved on and the panorama in the idyllic meadow turned along its own cosmic path.

~~ The End ~~

THE WHITE SKIFF

At mid-morning on Mother's Day Sunday the noise of an outboard motor cracked the stiff household silence, announcing the arrival of her husband's boss. He was towing a boat into their cove. Once she realized who it was, Marla had to put on the act. She had to pretend that she and Doug didn't have a nasty fight last night after his arrival home from a bar, angry and cursing her existence and at one point throwing her against the crib, breaking its gate. Marla's thick sweater would cover the bruises, but her mouth pulled downward making it hard to arrange the smiling mask she should wear for the occasion of the boat handover. Marla watched the boats from the single window in the two-room cabin with a heavy blankness in her mind like concrete had been poured inside herself.

Doug flew out of the bedroom and zipped up dirty jeans as he ran down to the cove. She watched him catch the tossed rope and tie the skiff to a low tree branch. Doug and Sturge exchanged words she could not hear, a brief conversation, and Sturge did not come ashore. He turned his own fiberglass cruiser around and drove right past the cabin's window, leaving a pale wake in the grey water of Puget Sound.

Marla knew that Sturge could see her standing at the window yet he did not wave back to her raised hand. Sturge was not a nice person, she reminded herself with a downbeat. He was grumpy, a man of few words and never a smile. She was the one who did the many can't-make-it-to-work-today phone calls to Sturge telling him that Doug wasn't feeling well. She knew and Sturge knew that Doug was a fuck-off. She knew, he knew--- those two thoughts formed an equation of deceit, an equation where the lie (n) equals truth as an impossibility (not n) by creating a sum of (1) lies to Sturge (the shame) plus (2) whenever she saw Sturge she disliked him even more (reminder of the shame). She was glad Sturge left. Glad! The skiff was theirs now. They had a boat! She could jig for cod. She could process the fish in canning jars if she had to. Clam chowder, she baby-talk whispered with excitement to Bethanny in the high chair. She had wheedled and needled to get that boat and now it was here.

The water turned to silver as the morning sun rose higher and the dark mounds far across the waters came into detail, the timbered islands. She watched a green and white ferry glide through a narrow pass between islands. It was the Vashon, coming from Friday Harbor and heading across her window view to the nearby Orcas Island ferry landing. Six ferries a day, more in the summer, and full of cars and passengers, these were her familiar sights and clockwork of sounds. She could hear the ferries dock, the bump against the pilings, the clang as the ramp came down and the speedway roar of all the cars starting up their engines.

Last night in the thick hours of midnight, the baby sleeping and Doug's usual absence --- he never came home direct from work anymore --- well after the last ferry departed she heard whales blowing in the Sound, orcas or humpbacks, huffing and spraying. What mystery and beauty to hear the sound of whales blowing. She ached to have Doug once again by her side, happy, and responding to her in a way that she did not fear; she would coax him into a walk down to the cove to listen, but he wasn't there. There was no moon that dark night yet the experience of hearing the whales was like receiving a tiny bright moon in the palm of her hand, something to always treasure.

She pushed aside thoughts of last night, its intensities and disappointments and got busy with household tasks. She made coffee for when Doug came back inside. She knew how it would go. He would drink coffee standing with his back to her; they would never speak of the argument as if pretending it away; and once again he would announce a reason he had to leave for the day. Everything they had together had become repulsive to him. He hated his job, he hated that they were a new family. She kept swallowing ugliness and cement, staying invisible, trying not to provoke him. Hot tears ran from her eyes and she wiped them away to make the face that doesn't look upset. She would have to keep that neutral look when Doug came back inside.

Their newly acquired boat had been used to check on rafts of logs in Bellingham Bay. Shaped more like a river boat, it was a kind of punt, made of plywood, broad-bottomed with a 40 horsepower outboard motor on the keel. A clumsy boat for salt water, nonetheless workable, sturdy, cheap. She never intended to go far with it, only down the shoreline for clams or about a hundred feet out from their cove to a certain cod hole she had fished once before with Doug's uncle when they first arrived, the spot now fixed in her memory by memorizing onshore markers, a particular tree, a neighbor's glass and metal mansion.

How they found out about the boat's availability was that Doug worked for Sturge's logging company. That boat had been brought out from Bellingham, tied up to a log boom on another island and during a storm had been swamped and sunk in shallow water. At a low tide Sturge had the boat hauled out and cleaned up, but after another hard look he didn't want it anymore. This was not the dreamy hand-hewn wooden skiff of the remarkable craftsman variety shown in boating magazines, rounded up to perfect points at the keel and bow with close fitted boards and all caulked and sanded to satin evenness, stained or painted with some inventive waterproof sealant out of an expensive can purchased at the chandlery, barnacle free and a vision of marine satin. Theirs was a slab boat painted white that she insisted on calling a skiff. So what! She was sticking with it.

When she walked with Bethanny down to the cove she saw too much of what was wrong. Plywood was showing through the paint. The keel panels were damaged, splintered. She wondered if a marine paint had been used, or if it was any old leftover paint. In the bottom of the boat there was an empty coffee can for bailing. At least there was a decent motor, an Evinrude. There was a short seat for the motor handler and two wide planks across the middle. The bow was squared, not brought to a fine point.

She had seen the boat of her dreams three times. Once in a library book. Once on Moran Lake, a beautiful honey-colored row boat owned by a sweet-natured octogenarian, and once up on saw horses while being crafted by a boatwright who wore bib overalls and had a long ponytail and Maori tattoos. What did all that matter, why did she remain obsessed with comparisons, a habit that put her inside a negativity box with no visible exit.

Their skiff would rest in the mud at low tide. She wanted to make an anchor weight and get an oar, but those were tasks she couldn't do alone. She would need money and gas in the pickup. He wouldn't give it to her, she knew that and she told herself to forget those ideas and live with the boat as they got it. She had to take it all like it was.

She went back inside the cabin, changed, fed, dressed Bethanny and placed her sweet girl in a table top seat while she made up the bed in the other room of the cabin. Everything always fluctuated between sweetness and vicious anger and she knew no in-betweens. Also, she did not know where Doug went. When he came inside a little while later, she realized that he had been in the driveway working on the pickup truck. His hands were dirty with motor oil. They didn't have hot water. He splashed hot water from the kettle into the dish basin and scrubbed his hands.

After his coffee and cereal Doug announced that they were all going to visit Eddie and Gretchen who lived in Apple Valley, a little hollow three miles into the interior of the island. Doug had to see Eddie to get something. Gretchen was lonely and wanted to meet Marla. She knew the Apple Valley house, knew it well, coveted that house, and was eager to see it again on the inside. She longed for a real house, not a rough-out fishing shack. Marla had been scoping out every rental possibility on Orcas Island. The cabin had become too small. A baby needs room to crawl and she didn't want Bethanny crawling in the driveway or in the mud, although Doug acted like that was a really funny possibility. He wouldn't take anything about the baby seriously. She had lost her sense of humor, the rage munched it up and all she could give was a half smile at the thought. He refused to understand that the hot stove in the middle of the tiny front room could burn a crawling infant. He had shrugged and walked away with dismissive remark that she spent too much time thinking about how other people did things. She silenced herself because it made him angry and she couldn't find the way out of the dilemma. Why did he never come home? Why did he hate her so much? He needed her to make the phone calls to Sturge, to the landlord (rent would be late) and what else, to beat on. She was going insane thinking like this in rounds of rationalization, as if her thoughts swirled like marbles in a can. She didn't think Doug even remembered her name anymore. He acted squirmy and embarrassed to have the baby in his arms. He hated giving her money for food. These thoughts she held to herself like a bandage wrapped too tight on a wound.

She inquired what he had to get from Eddie. She didn't really know that couple, had only spoken a few words to them at the post office. Doug barely turned to tell her that a part was needed for the pickup truck, the carburetor and Eddie had one to sell.

She readied herself and Bethanny and off they went to the Apple Valley house that the owners refused to rent to Doug, a puzzle she could not unravel. How bizarre that she was going to visit the new tenants, a couple the same age as themselves and with a toddler too. It was unfair. They should have got that house. Doug had a good job with Sturge and she heard that Eddie didn't even have a job. Doug's family had homesteaded on the island, they went back that far. Marla was an import here herself and was shocked by the indifference of Doug's family and the cold currents that ran beneath the small community.

The damn pickup always needed something, oil, belt, tires. She readied herself and Bethanny and off they went, looking like a Mother's Day family excursion in the bright noon sun, zooming down the road, a turn to go down into the valley and a hard right onto the smooth driveway of the house she wanted and couldn't have.

Clapboard. Two stories, pale blue. There was a back porch, a wonderful roofed back porch where there could be a washing machine, a baby bouncer, a place to stand and drink coffee in the morning and look out on orchards and deer.

Gretchen welcomed them warmly while plaiting her hair into braids. Their son Amos was walking and talking, a center of attention. The two women stood at the kitchen table (there were no chairs) and chatted about children while the men went to see about an abandoned flatbed truck parked in the tall grass on the backside of a shed.

Gretchen showed off some of the rooms of the house, not all, some doors were closed. There was very little furniture. She explained that she didn't like the place because it seemed to echo with old violence, especially one particular downstairs bedroom. She led Marla to the bad room where their voices echoed from dingy walls, wooden floors, an open closet. The room's bare windows faced the road and mirrored themselves, two women with long faces. Amos ran circles inside the room. Gretchen pointed to a huge grey stain on one wall. See how big the stain is? I think it's blood. Maybe someone shot themselves in this room. Marla thought it looked like coffee, like they heaved a coffee mug in anger and suggested wallpaper to cover it.

Too pricey. Right now we're broke, Gretchen admitted, and we don't have any food. That's our priority for today. Come see. I'll show you. Back in the kitchen Gretchen held up the smallest can of evaporated milk Marla had ever seen. It looked like a sample. That's all we have, absolutely all. Gretchen opened all the kitchen cupboard doors displaying barren shelves but for a few cups, drinking glasses, plates. The two women laughed about Mother Hubbard. No bones!

Yet something about having no food at all frightened Marla because this couple had a child. And they did not move in yesterday. They had been there several months. Eddie was an architect. So that's what the landlord liked. Eddie promised to fix up the place. Gretchen said he was slow to come out of the planning stage and he had lots of drawings. She gestured toward rolls of paper on the floor of the living room. Right now they didn't have electricity but they planned to have it turned on soon. They didn't have a couch but they had a line on one, maybe they could get it soon. Empty cupboards, not even Krusteez pancake mix. The house was so empty that it seemed this family floated like dandelion fluff, wisping through the air and living on the breeze. Minimalist, Gretchen joked, that's what our architect has decreed. Amos and I sit on the mattress in the bedroom or play outside when the day is warm.

Gretchen offered tea from chamomile she had picked in their driveway. I don't cook, she shrugged. We eat a lot of PB and J and bananas. We're out of that. As soon as the guys do the deal, she added, we are going into Eastsound for burgers and to buy groceries. I wish they would hurry. Marla made a move to go ask Doug to hurry up. Gretchen held her arm. Don't bother them. They're doing a deal.

Marla was taken aback by Gretchen's choice of words. She placated by stating that a carburetor can take a long time to remove. Gretchen laughed, Eddie doesn't know a thing about cars! He wouldn't know a carburetor from toaster. He's the architect who doesn't own a hammer, Mister Big Talker. He can draw, that was his last job, doing renderings for a big architectural firm in Seattle. He never got his degree, one more class, that's all he needed, four credits, and he wouldn't do it. I got money from my father and here we are, end of the road and all that, staying clean. There is so much to do in this house that it bores me. I think about what we have to do but I cannot begin anything. Everything requires we buy something so forget it. That's the way it goes every day, and every day slips by.

Minimalist is easier. Marla shook her head up and down, struggling with a rising uncertainty.

Eddie can't keep a job. He's got a problem. He will do anything for jack. Not for me, but for jack.

Who's Jack?

Jack off, you know. H. Her son was holding onto her leg. She picked him up and Amos snuggled into her neck, closing his eyes. Gretchen swayed slowly as Amos slept. They want thirty dollars deposit for the lights can you believe. Where are we going to get that. The only time I ever had money was when my father gave me the cash. It was mine anyway, he owed me from when my mother died. He didn't go to the funeral so busy with his new family. I asked and he gave me money. I left his office and went from shop to shop like a madwoman, grabbing this and that, I mean anything that caught my eye, dresses, jewelry, lingerie, grabbing this and that like a madwoman because Eddie was waiting with Amos in the city parking lot and he was going to take all that cash away from me. I hid most of the stuff in my big purse and said the rest was a gift. I only had so much time to spend that money, my money. Two thousand dollars. Between my father's office and the parking lot I managed to spend one thousand getting pretty things for me, only me. I love spending. She moaned in a long exhale, we'll never see that much money again. I bought everything I saw that was pretty, she repeated. And the rest was I gave to Eddie. You know how he spent it? He threw it away, no surprise, believe me. Threw it away.

He spent a thousand dollars on what?

He bought H. He always finds it. I had to return some of my stuff so we could come up here from Seattle. Orcas is all right for the end of the road. It's green. We needed a new start, clean, the basics, go to the islands and hunker down, so we thought. Eddie got pretty sick when there was no more H and we didn't have ferry fare to go get more. We stayed inside and he went cold, cleaned out, and he was nearly dead before he got done. That was a horrible time for me. I thought he would die and I would have to tell everybody about it. I got scared and creeped out and I had Amos to take care of and the whole week was all about Eddie's misery, his puking, his sweating, his groaning. I never want to go through that again. If he doesn't give me money for food today I'm leaving him and going back to Seattle. We've broken up once before; this time could be for real. I have enough for the ferry for me and Amos.

The men came inside the house and leaned against the kitchen counters. Doug had a foolish grin on his face. She could smell the pot they had smoked, something she had given up more than a year ago before she got pregnant. She looked at Eddie without making eye contact. He was very thin. Within minutes it was arranged that Eddie and Gretchen would come to their cabin after they went to the grocery store in Eastsound and go for a ride in the skiff.

It's not a real skiff, it's a slab boat, Doug corrected, made of plywood. Marla suggested that they dress very warm because it's colder on the water and the wind can come up in the afternoon. No one listened to her. They didn't have life jackets. It'll be all right, the three countered Marla's concern. We won't go out far. The conversation weakened into goodbyes as she and Doug went down the porch steps. Marla put her hand on the porch column, lingering for long beautiful seconds to take in the whole valley, its apple trees with stick winter limbs about to burst into bloom and the sunken hollow of the land between hills visible in its soft cupping. Winter almost over.

As Doug drove home, she asked about the carburetor, if it was hard to remove from the flatbed. Doug laughed that

Eddie didn't have any tools and he didn't bring any. Instead he sold Doug some pot instead. He'd been growing plants in some rooms using lights.

Marla hid her surprise. She turned her head and leaned against the passenger window which was warm from the sun. She didn't react outwardly. All she could think about was strangled plants that never knew the sun, fixating on the idea of sun-deprived greenery.

She couldn't bear to look at him for when she did waves of fear surged over her and she thought she was going crazy. He had wasted their rent money on pot. She worked too. She carried Bethanny four miles three times a week to a small resort at West Beach where she cleaned rooms and toilets for a mean woman with big teeth who thought Marla was untrustworthy. It was the lowest Marla had ever been, silent, groveling and scrubbing and she had to do it every Friday, Saturday and Monday afternoons. Bethanny stayed with a woman in a house just past the resort. Nothing was ever going to change. Everything was collapsing inward. What would happen to Bethanny if she, Marla, broke into little pieces, she couldn't, and wherever the glue came from she had to hold herself together.

At mid-afternoon everybody got into the boat. Doug pushed off and the rope trailed in the water. Marla noticed that nobody else reached to pull the rope out of the water. She handed Bethanny to Gretchen and stretched to get all the rope into the boat. She placed the bailing can beside the coiled rope at her feet. The motor roared. The air flew in their faces. She and Gretchen sat together holding their children snug. Doug handled the motor and Eddie seemed dazed. Up close the salt water of Puget Sound lapped very cold and very deep. There was no bottom, her thoughts slid into death and she fought mentally against rising fear. Survival was measured in minutes in cold water. Anyone overboard had minutes to swim to shore before hypothermia numbed and sank them to the bottom. No one in the boat knew her thoughts. Gretchen pulled on her sleeve and brought her back to Bethanny's smile. The children were happy. She concentrated on the water's sparkle, the glassy expanse, the reflections.

They floated offshore in front of the cabin in about twenty feet of water. She felt assured. This was satisfactory. The boat was sound. A little more floating, enjoying the motion in the water, the light bobbing and the giggles of Amos, all were smiling. That was enough! There was a nice view, everything looked green and silvery, wet and clean. Ten minutes of this and they could go back to shore, return to the cove, eat thick sliced home baked bread with blackberry jam and drink hot rose hip tea, warming up.

The men decided to run the boat across the channel to Lopez Island. Gretchen and Marla looked into each other's eyes with dread. The boat turned, the motor roared and they drew a big wake as they aimed directly across to the distant hump of green. The wind whipped Marla's hot face and she burrowed little Bethany deep inside the blanket. Gretchen and Amos were laughing as they were splashed with cold water when Doug zigzagged the boat for fun.

The water was calm, a saving grace. In the distance there were other boats, cabin cruisers, a sailboat, a fishing boat, quite far away. Emerald humps of islands rose from the silver waters. They approached the far tip of Lopez Island when a huge ferry suddenly bore down Wasp Pass. Doug cut the motor. They could see a beach quite a ways off. A rocky reef appeared inches below the water, an unexpected barrier between the skiff and the beach. Marla reached out and touched the sharp-edged brown rock as the enormous ferry glided within a few feet of their boat, its sides rising four stories high. They had been in its path as the ferry made a turn out of Wasp Pass to head across to the Orcas landing. Passengers watched from the heights of an observation deck. There were deck hands up there also, and she watched a few of them untying a life boat. The ferry proceeded past them, cutting through the water and displacing large quantities of the water which moved toward them in undulations.

The skiff rocked side to side. Gretchen screamed at Eddie to sit down when he stood up and said he would push them off from the side of the ferry, which was too far away to touch. They leaned opposites to steady the rocking. Marla bailed quickly. The rocking panicked Gretchen and she was crying. Amos began crying also and Bethanny joined in with infant screaming. Why had the ferry turned so close to their skiff? Maybe the pilot didn't see them, maybe they were too small. The reef held them fixed like a rough brown hand rising from the deep. Marla reached into the icy water and pushed off from the rough rock. She measured the distance to the beach if the boat capsized and planned how she would hold Bethanny close to one shoulder while she swam with the other hand. It would be difficult to swim because of shoes and layers of clothing but she could do it. Doug yelled at her to bail faster rapidly as more water spilled into the boat.

Once the ferry passed, rolls of big water from its wake lifted them up and down into troughs. Gunning the Evinrude, Doug maneuvered the outboard engine away from the reef, across the long lumpy lines of diminishing wake, and across the broad endless channel, aiming for the cove, the sooner the better. The beauty of Puget Sound on a sunny day receded into oblivion. All silver turned to gray and all sparkle became wicked.

They had taken a tremendous and dangerous chance with the children in the boat. Impetuous and stupid, nothing to laugh about but the men started laughing. Marla was sweating as she and Gretchen calmed the children with soothing words. All had survived yet they still had to cross the channel. Marla hugged Gretchen, who was crying and angry at the same time. Gretchen hissed between her teeth that if they got to shore she was leaving Eddie for good this time. She would never let him do this to them again. Amos clung to Gretchen and Bethanny began crying again.

Halfway across the channel the boat motor died. Doug got it re-started, although its lawnmower-like noise stopped again making a profound silence on the water. When he got the hood off the outboard motor and began tinkering with parts, he accidentally dropped the screwdriver into the water. It sank forever. The moment he dropped the tool, Marla's love for Doug sank into the cold water, gone forever. She hated Doug with an intensity that shattered her inner blankness. The concrete crumbled and released a certainty. She would never forgive his careless, carefree, easy way he disregarded her and Bethanny. Love, altered forever.

After much penknife-scraping of sparkplugs and blowing through gas lines, Doug and Eddie did get the motor steadily roaring. They proceeded across the channel and halted twice more with the overworked faulty motor. Each time the engine roar restarted, Gretchen encouraged Amos to yell hooray. Marla stared with fixation on Orcas Island as if pulling an invisible rope. Marla knew she had witnessed a force of fate that sideswiped their excursion, brought them all to the edge of disaster, and then cast them aside like a wind looking for other interests. That's how they all became survivors — because it sure wasn't anything they did for themselves. Doug doesn't try to protect us. Like Gretchen, her day of departure was looming. Doug had put her baby in danger once in anger and once on a whim. There! She could now describe the certainty that had become resident inside her now its cement casing shattered.

At the cove everybody got out of the skiff pretty fast. Gretchen hustled Amos to their car; there would be no lingering over bread and jam. Eddie hunkered with Doug at the edge of the cove to smoke part of a joint before Eddie remembered Gretchen and Amos and said his goodbyes and drove away.

Marla was now faced with the habitual routine of a bitter household. Her plans of escape kept falling apart. It would take eight weeks, more beatings, and the unexpected help of two strangers, the couple from the glass and metal house — they assisted her furtive departure with Bethanny. The hardest part was revealing to those two people the truth of her violent marriage on the night she escaped from a horrible beating with Bethanny wrapped in a crib blanket and, fortuitously, her purse. When Marla realized she couldn't stay all night in the cold wet woods. She knocked on the massive door of the glass and metal house and asked them to hide her for the night before she could get on the sunrise ferry. The humiliation and begging crushed her and it was by holding Bethanny that she found fierce courage.

The couple provided so much and with only a few questions.

She never saw them again.

They were like the unseen captain of the ferry who finally took heed of the skiff and piloted very slowly on the turn out of Wasp Pass to lessen the wake.

It would be a Mother's Day decades later while playing on a carpet in a large living room with a happy grandchild, some toy boats, and a different husband that she recalled this excursion from long ago, a sudden memory ping! Like finding the last pieces of a puzzle, she realized with a wholeness and with humility what the captain of the ferry and what the couple in the glass and metal house had done to extend her life and possibly the life of her child. Time stretched far behind her. After a bit she recalled the strange story of Eddie and Gretchen. She wondered about Doug who she never heard from again. He did not show up at the divorce court proceedings and the judge reprimanded her for not making him come there, an admonishment she absorbed in silence.

She had long regarded her long-ago life on the island as a blurry contrast to the present, dark and medium grey. It was finally in focus. A thick rising of anger had overwhelmed the clarity of love, first marriage love, in her heart. Grasping for rope in cold water, hoping against hope by calling the slab boat a skiff, and finally, the territory of safety. The summation of all those parts made her life into a complex equation where a symbol of infinity represented compassion. All the factors plus all the figures and boats were multiplied by time to formulate a bobbing balance upon a roaring sea.

~~ The End ~~

SPIRIT CHIEF

The Chief sat in the driveway, a pale Chevy pickup truck that had never been waxed nor frequently washed but whose engine had been admired and maintained with thoughtful attention. Now it was 65 years old and a little tired. Nonetheless, there were hills that The Chief would attack in first gear with the strength of vengeance and a war whoop, forgetting age and remembering only victory. "Not yet will I die, you old miserable hill! Watch me stride to the top," growled The Chief. "I have been to the woods and nothing surprises me anymore."

Decals of famous Indian chiefs were pasted on the dashboard. Two insulated wires hung semi-permanently beneath the steering wheel, for manual ignition. To start the pickup both exposed copper wire ends were twisted together This connecting of wires ignited the motor. The sounds of the motor starting were strong, raspy and snorty. The Chief and his war horse engine were one.

In the fall and winter, and sometimes wet springs and cool summers, the skies were grey and overcast all day. Cold rain drizzled when it didn't pour. Streaks of steam and condensation fogged the windows inside and out so the best way to back out of a muddy, rutted driveway lined with trees was to roll down the driver's window and lean out, looking backwards and keeping the right hand on the steering wheel.

In the land of Evermore fortunately the hearts of trucks remain long after their tires are removed and their bodies compressed into cubes of steel. Like ghosts folded into shipping boxes, their colored smoky forms emerge on nights when the moon is full and the dark highways and woody roads glisten with fresh rain. These forms unfold from the cubes and stretch like horses and cats, eyeing a horizon where any way is exciting and possible.

They appear to test the air and paw the earth; then without further fuss the colored, shapely forms race along great unwinding lengths of black satin. They voraciously pass any solid motorists, leaving the impression of a rocking blast of sudden wind.

"What was that?" drivers ask their companions in the front seat. "That was some gust! Felt like a truck, didn't it?"

~~ The End ~~

Dedicated to the memory of Leona Harvich
aka Druezelda Hardy, artist, friend and bright treasure

The author, Penny Sidoli, lives on the wet western edge of the North American continent. This is her first collection of short stories. One day while driving slow on a lonely dirt road in the open country west of Albuquerque, within the southwest region of the Navajo Nation, she stopped to enjoy the sight of wild horses running and noticed this sign:

Hoping to meet you someday at the intersection of Daydream and Driving Slow ...